THE SORCER

BOOK TWO OF THE K

Robert Ryan

Cover design by www.damonza.com

ISBN: 9798664526530
(print edition)

Trotting Fox Press

Contents

1. A Shadow of Dark Magic

Faran drifted on a wave of magic.

He did not know where he was, for in the void there was no *where*. Nor was there a *when*. He merely was, and he floated on currents of time and space that were but echoes of the real world.

It was a lonely place. Yet it was peaceful also. Here, he might contemplate a speck of dust for eons to unravel its mysteries. Or he might cast out his mind to encompass the vast cosmos and grasp its secrets in a single moment. It was all the same, in the end.

His mind felt stretched, as though these thoughts were too big for it. Yet thoughts had no size, so there was no limit to what his mind could perceive. If there was a wall there, he had built it himself.

Something changed, and he felt a sensation of falling.

Down he dropped, plummeting. And memory came back to him of where he had been.

Within the standing stones he had stood, that circle of monuments from another age. Aranloth had invoked their magic. Traveling, it was called. By doing so they had escaped Lindercroft as their enemy was on the cusp of capturing them. Or more likely, killing them.

But even as the sensation of falling increased, Faran remembered one other thing. At the very last moment, some creature of dark magic had leaped within the circle and Traveled with them.

It was here now, in the void. It was falling with him, and its purpose was to kill him. There was no question of that. And it could move with blinding speed.

Faran felt his bow in his hand. Before the magic of the stones commenced, he had been preparing to loose an arrow and defend himself. But the creature had been coming for him, and he knew that he would not be quick enough.

Had anything changed? He felt reality swiftly approaching, and expected to be torn and shredded by the terrible claws and teeth that he had seen.

A brilliant light burst against his eyes, and then, swift as it had come, it faded away into oblivion.

He was left where he had been when the magic commenced, in a ring of standing stones.

No. These stones were taller and grander. They had Traveled, as Aranloth said they would.

His bow felt heavy in his hand. The dark shadow of the creature streaked toward him. Aranloth was straightening from where he had been stooping to activate the magic. Kareste was turning from where she had been looking at Lindercroft.

Faran held his bow before him as a protection against the creature that now leaped at his throat. It was too late to loose an arrow. But suddenly, out of nowhere, Ferla was there.

Ferla, her red hair flying behind her, launched herself at the creature. She had drawn no knife, but instead used her own body as a weapon.

There was a thump as the two bodies met. The creature grunted in surprise and Ferla cried out, and then she rebounded as her slight body collided with the much larger.

She fell down as though she had hurled herself against a wall, and yet, for all the creature's size, her intervention had thrown it off balance.

Teeth flashing and claws gleaming, it twisted in the air and landed to Faran's left even as he dodged to the right.

He was amazed at his friend's courage, but her bravery had not saved him.

The creature scrambled over the ground, claws tearing up chunks of dirt, and then its dark eyes fixed at Faran's throat and it leaped again.

This time, he had the opportunity to loose his arrow. It sped over the few feet that separated him from his attacker and drove into its chest.

The shaft penetrated deep, taking the creature square on and sending it tumbling to the side. Part wolf it seemed, and part man. Faran had no name for it, but he sensed it was a thing born of deep magic.

Whatever it was, it was strong. It reared up now on two legs, and a deep-throated growl tore the air. It was not a growl of pain, but of anger. Again it came at Faran, this time sprinting at him.

Faran loosed another arrow, but the creature swerved and dodged it. Kareste now joined the fray, a streak of brilliant blue flame leaping from her staff and pummeling the beast. Even as it reeled from that, Aranloth was there also. At a wave of his staff, a silver-white wall of flame leaped up between Faran and his attacker.

But the creature was not done. It rolled to the ground, snapping the arrow that protruded from its chest, and it lurched upright once more, patches of its dark fur smoldering with remnants of blue flame. It leaped again.

Faran reeled back, and the beast leaped into Aranloth's wall of flame. That wall bent under the creature's weight, and Faran, fearful nothing would stop the creature trying to kill him, fumbled to nock another arrow.

The silver-white wall bent, but held. Then it folded back over the creature, enveloping it. Aranloth had made it to do so, and with a sweep of his staff he sent more lòhren-fire at it to shore up the weak spots of his trap.

Ferla was standing again, and she worked her bow, speeding several arrows into the creature.

Faran followed her example. Coolly now, he stood his ground and sped arrows, one after another, with rapid movements that only long practice could hone.

He could not be sure how effective this was. The arrows burned even as they pierced the lòhren-fire, but the darkened shafts streaked into that deadly trap and, if nothing else, the metal heads struck the creature. It turned and twisted, seeming to bite itself in response to the pain they caused.

But it did not die. Its black eyes fixed once more on Faran, and he felt the cold wind of death blow upon him. The thing howled, and though there was terrible agony in its voice, there was not yet weakness. This thing would come for him until its last breath, if a thing of such dark magic even breathed.

The beast strained against the bonds that held it, ignoring the fiery touch of Aranloth's magic and looking like it would leap out of its confinement and rend Faran's flesh.

Kareste took a few paces closer. Now, each arrow that Ferla sped into the creature the lòhren infused with her own magic.

The arrows flew, flaring with blue light and piercing the chest of the creature. It reared and howled, those blue arrows sticking from its chest, and they continued to burn long after the wood that made them must have turned to ash.

Enveloped by white flame, pierced by blue lòhren-fire that burned from within, at last the creature staggered.

Yet, summoning its last strength, it bunched its muscles and leaped again. The white magic about it bent and shredded, and it tumbled from its trap, a thing of snapping teeth, razor-sharp claws and smoking fur burned in places to expose blackened flesh.

It fell, rose again, and scrambled toward Faran setting the grass afire where its massive paws trod the ground.

Ferla strode closer, and she loosed an arrow straight at the creature's head. Kareste's magic touched the shaft in flight, and it penetrated an eye and drove deep into the brain.

The beast screamed, and it reared up on two legs again. Faran sent an arrow into its throat, and slowly, like a fallen tree, it toppled to the ground.

There it lay, trembling and panting, its hind legs twitching as life ebbed away. Faran looked into the remaining eye, and beyond the signs of agony he saw surprise and the fear of death. In pity, he drew one more arrow and loosed it into the creature, seeking its heart.

The arrow sped home, and the creature went limp. Faran turned away then, overcome by a strange grief at the death of an enemy that would have killed him. Tears stung his eyes, and the stench of burned flesh wafted through the air, making him gag.

"Look!" Ferla cried, and he swung back. Even as he did so the body of the beast writhed and twisted, turning to smoke as the dark magic that held it together unraveled.

But that was not all. Within the smoke a vision formed. It was a man, like Lindercroft, though older. His hair was silver, and on his head was a crown.

"The king," Aranloth said softly. Then more loudly, "Beware! Magic is unleashed!"

Light flared and then subsided. The king reeled, as though in pain, and perhaps that was so. The king wished Faran dead, so it may have been his dark sorcery that sent the beast rather than Lindercroft's. If so, would the summoner of such a creature remain connected by magic to it? Would its death bring pain?

But there was no time to think of such things, still less how a vision of the king came to be formed. That he was there was what mattered, and he regained his composure and turned to look at them with bloodshot eyes, one by one.

Faran was disturbed. If Lindercroft had seemed a man of power, how much more so the king? His eyes bored into everything they saw like driven nails. Authority draped him like a cloak, and even Faran sensed the aura of sorcery that enveloped him, greater by far than the power of kings.

Those bloodshot eyes turned to Aranloth. "We meet again, Nuatha. For so I now call you. Aranloth is not a name we respect anymore."

Aranloth, despite being a figure of legend, older by far and more powerful than the king, looked nothing like him. He leaned casually against his staff, as though crowns and dark sorcery were nothing to him.

"Names mean little to me, Druilgar. I have forgotten more of mine than you have ever had. But the title of Guide, of Osahka, is important. To me at least. It *means* something. Do you tell me that it means nothing now to you?"

The king frowned. "The title remains important. It is a name of honor and respect. But I now bestow that honor on another. I learn deeper of the mysteries than you would ever have taught me, and I am content. Do not seek to undermine that, for it is stronger by far than the bond we ever shared."

"If you say so," Aranloth answered.

"I *do* say so," the king said, and if he did not raise his voice there was still a tone of anger in it.

"Who now is Osahka to you, Druilgar? Do not say the Morleth Stone itself. That would be no bond. That would be a chain."

"Ah, you seek to provoke me. By trying to make me angry you hope I will reveal more of what I know and how I learned it. But I have no time for childish games."

Aranloth laughed, but there was little humor in the sound.

"I know whence your power comes, and your knowledge. I knew these things before your ancestors ever thought of traveling east and founding cities such as Faladir. I know also that high as you may rise under the influence of the stone, your fall will come also, and it will be hard for you."

The king paled, though whether in fear or anger was not obvious.

"You know nothing," he said quietly. "Less than nothing. Have you ever held the stone and invoked its power?"

Aranloth shook his head. "No, for I know its origin. I would not use the thing even at great need. It would—"

"Enough! You have never used it, and you do not understand it. Perhaps you lacked the courage. But I have, and I have leaned things you would never have taught me."

The lòhren shrugged. "I'm no more, or less, courageous than most people. But this is not about courage. It's about wisdom, and one day you will remember my words."

"You tried before to anger me. Now, you try to plant the seed of doubt. But I am beyond your manipulations. Are you, though, beyond mine?"

The king shifted his gaze, and Faran felt the force of those bloodshot eyes again.

"This is the pitiful man you would raise against me? Do you really think hc has it in him to fulfil prophecy?"

Aranloth grinned. "Who is really the pitiful one? You tell me that you will try to manipulate me, but really what you seek is information."

The king inclined his head. "Then tell me straight out. Is he the seventh knight?"

The lòhren ran a hand through his hair as though in thought.

"A fair question, and so I'll give you a fair answer. No, I don't think he is."

The king sighed. "I should have known better than to bother. You never could answer a straight question with a simple answer. But lying is beneath you."

The king glanced at Faran again. "Tell me this, if Aranloth will not. Are you the seventh knight?"

Faran felt the weight of those bloodshot eyes, and he sensed what he should not in a king. Evil. It was one thing to be told that this man was ultimately responsible for the destruction of Dromdruin Village, but it was another to see him face to face, and to feel the truth of it.

"I'm not the seventh knight. I don't care what anyone says or thinks – that's not me. But this much is true, and I said it to Lindercroft, and now I say it to you. I'll hunt you down for destroying my village. And I'll kill you for it."

The king seemed startled, but he smoothed over his features swiftly.

"Bold words, and maybe Aranloth has chosen better than I thought. You have the makings of a knight. Or at least the courage of one. Sadly, we'll never know. You are marked for death, and it will find you. Not as swiftly as I had desired, but swift enough."

The gaze of the king then fell to Ferla, and he made to speak. But Aranloth acted first.

"This conversation is done, Druilgar." Raising his staff, the lòhren called forth a gust of wind that shredded the image of the king and sent it into oblivion.

"None too soon," Kareste said. "I was growing tired of him. The knights have indeed fallen."

Aranloth did not answer. He seemed preoccupied. Faran looked around in the silence that ensued. This was a greater ring of standing stones than the one they had left near Nurthil Wood.

The stones were just as old, made ragged by the passage of time, but the circle itself was larger and the stones themselves were half as tall again.

There was something not quite right here, though. It felt odd, and an uneasiness that he could not explain crept up on him.

He looked out for the first time beyond the stones. The sun was high in the sky, and the afternoon was drawing on. But the light was good, and what he saw stretching out for mile after mile surprised him. Everywhere he looked were ruins. This had once been a vast city. So vast that it must have dwarfed even Faladir.

The ring of stones was on a hill, and Faran gazed down on the remnants of a long-forgotten city. Perhaps that was what was making him uneasy, for it was hard not to think of mortality in the face of that. Millions of people must have lived here on a time, and they were all dead now.

He turned to look at Aranloth. Perhaps not all were dead. But the lòhren seemed unwell. His brown robes shimmered, and they became white. He must have been using the same sort of magic that Kareste had done before to disguise his appearance.

Why that should be, Faran did not know. They knew now who he was. Perhaps the illusion was to disguise himself from others they met or that would see them from a distance.

“Best to be gone from here,” the old man said. “There’s still daylight left and time to walk several miles.”

But even as they crossed the threshold of the stones, Aranloth stumbled. If not for his staff, he would have fallen. And as he lurched, Faran saw what looked like a shadow detach from him and lengthen away down the hill. But that was not possible, so he ignored it.

2. The Arts of the Knights

Kareste rushed to Aranloth's side and put an arm around him. He tottered for a moment, and then straightened, a terrible look in his eyes.

What had just happened, Faran was not sure. But whatever afflicted the old man passed swiftly. He gave a shrug and then spoke in a steady voice that was reassuring.

"Don't mind me. Traveling is never easy, and it can cause strange … feelings. I'll be fine in a moment or two."

"Let's sit and rest for a little while," Kareste suggested.

There was a tumbled wall nearby, the remnant of some sort of building, and they moved over to that and found some knee-high stones to sit on.

Aranloth did seem fine now, and he looked about him alertly, so Faran decided to ask some questions.

"Where, exactly, have we Traveled to?"

Aranloth sighed. "What you see now are ruins, but once this was the greatest city ever built. It had many names, but Tallach-far was one of the most widely known. This is the heart of the Letharn empire that was. Here, emperors and empresses ruled a dominion that stretched leagues beyond count and into lands that are lost to history. As is this city." He looked back at the ring of standing stones and then continued. "In a matter of moments, we have Traveled some hundred miles south of where we started."

Faran considered that. It was near impossible to understand, but he had felt the magic. And the land was so different here that what the lòhren said must be true.

"Why come here? Could we have gone anywhere?"

"That's not how the stones work. Few Rings were ever built, and some no longer function. But it's only possible to Travel from one Ring to another. There were other places I could have chosen, but this one will serve us well."

That all seemed to make sense to Faran. Something worried him though.

"Is it possible that Lindercroft could follow us, or learn where we went?"

Aranloth grinned. "He would be a very angry man right now, and I can live with that. He does not know how the standing stones work. He cannot use them. He just knows that we escaped him, and that he will have to answer for it to Druilgar, who is not known to be forgiving. I can live with that, too."

Faran studied the lòhren carefully. He seemed alert and well on the surface, but underneath were signs of tiredness and strain. Strange that he should show it now for the first time. What had changed?

Kareste was also looking at him, and Faran saw worry on her face. At least he thought he did, but the moment he seemed to notice it her face became like a mask and showed nothing.

"Why don't you and Ferla talk among yourselves for a while. Aranloth could do with some rest by himself."

Faran stood up from the stone he was sitting on. The worry may have been gone from her face, but her words betrayed it. She usually referred to Aranloth lightly as the *old man*. Just now, she had used his name.

But she was right. He did need rest, and Faran moved away with Ferla to another portion of the wall some distance away.

"You did it again," he said to her when they had seated themselves.

"Did what?"

"Saved my life. That … thing would have had me. And I haven't even asked if you're hurt."

"Do I look like I'm hurt?"

He shook his head. "No, but I should have asked. I'm sorry."

"Well, I'm one ahead at the moment. I've saved you twice, and you've saved me once. You'd better take your chance to catch up when you get the opportunity." She winked at him to let him know it was a joke.

He grinned in return. But he could not help feel that by the time all this was over he would have that chance, and the thought saddened him. She should not be at risk because of him.

The circumstances were beyond his control though, and she would not leave. In turn, he knew if the situation were reversed, he would not leave her. There was nothing to be done about it, so he changed the subject.

"Did you see anything … unusual when Aranloth stumbled before?"

She gave him a sharp look. "Maybe. I'm not sure. What did *you* see?"

He chose his words carefully. "I'm not sure either. I *thought* that I saw some sort of shadow just glide away from him. It was very strange."

"I think," she answered slowly, "that I saw the same thing. It was just from the corner of my eye, and I thought I must have imagined it. But maybe not if you saw it too."

He looked away. It seemed they had both seen something, but neither could be certain. And both of them feared that if they were right, it could only be one thing. Magic. But whose?

"Do you think Lindercroft managed to send something after us?" he asked.

She shook her head. "Aranloth just said before that we escaped him. He seemed certain of it. So I don't see how it could be anything to do with him."

Faran was not quite so sure. What if Aranloth was wrong? Still, if the magic was Lindercroft's doing, would he not have sent something to attack them instead?

"Then what was it?"

"I don't know, Faran. Maybe it didn't even happen, and we only thought we saw something."

"That could be. Maybe. But promise me this, anyway. Keep your eyes open. Watch out for anything strange."

She flicked back a strand of dark red hair that blew across her face.

"Everything has been strange lately. But I know what you mean. We'll both stay alert."

They talked quietly for a little while longer. The afternoon sun slanted a little more, sending long shadows down from the hill. But soon Kareste called them over.

"We can rest and eat at the same time," she said.

They broke open some of the new supplies they had received in Nurthil Wood, and ate a late lunch or an early dinner.

Aranloth seemed his normal self, although there were purple-blue rings around his eyes that had not been there earlier. Faran ate a chunk of dark bread, quite different from the loaves made in Dromdruin. It was heavy and dry, but it did have a deep flavor.

"That bread will last longer than normal bread," Aranloth said. "It's made for traveling, and it's smoked and salted. The knights use it when they travel the realm."

Kareste was chewing vigorously on some. "It might be made for travel, but it certainly isn't made for good flavor."

"You might acquire a taste for it." He reached out and broke a chunk off the loaf for himself. "I have, and normal bread just seems like empty air once you get used to this."

Kareste made a face. "I've tasted better, old man. But if I live to be your age, who can say how strange my tastes might become?"

Aranloth laughed, and Faran was glad to see it. It seemed like the weight of the world had been lifted from the lòhren's shoulders, and that was reassuring. Without him, they might all be dead by now.

But the old man's face grew serious again, and he glanced at Faran shrewdly.

"We're safe," he said, "at least for the moment. Lindercroft has lost us, and not even the elù-drak that serve him have much chance of finding us now. At least for a long time."

"But?" replied Faran.

"You know what I'm trying to say."

Faran drew a deep breath. "I know. We're safe just now, but that doesn't mean Lindercroft, or the king, will give up the hunt. They never will. I don't like it, but it's true. None of this situation was of my making, but the sooner I accept it, the better."

The old man did not answer that. No answer could be given. But it felt good to Faran to admit out loud the way he had been feeling. And there was something else that he had realized as well.

"You've done a lot for me." He turned to face Kareste also. "And you as well. Without the both of you, Ferla and I would be dead. I don't have the skills needed to keep myself alive against the enemies that hunt me. That has to change." He looked back at Aranloth. "Legend says you were the tutor of the knights. Will you teach me what I need to stay alive? Will you teach me how to protect myself?"

The old man looked at him solemnly. "Yes. I'll teach you. But it will need to be more than the martial skills of the knights alone."

"Because," Faran said reluctantly, "the enemies who will come against me possess magic?"

"Indeed they will. Things of terrible and dark sorcery such as you have never seen."

"But I'm no lòhren to wield such powers."

Aranloth gazed at him thoughtfully. "Perhaps not, yet even the least of the knights learned magic, of a sort. You have it in you to learn more. And you will need more."

The old man paused, as though deciding whether or not to say something now that he had considered before.

"To that end, you will need fitting armor. And a fitting blade. These must be made to fulfil not just the dints of battle, but the blows of magic."

Faran thought on that. It was more than he had asked, but how else did one defend against enemies such as he had?

"These things that we're talking about are the weapons, armor and skills of a Kingshield Knight," he said at length.

Aranloth nodded silently.

"And will you still allow all this," Faran continued, "even if I'm not, nor will ever become, a Kingshield Knight?"

"Even so."

The lòhren's swift answer was reassuring. But Faran wanted more.

"Why?"

"Because it is right. And because your grandfather was a good man. But mostly because you will need these things to live."

Faran nodded. He felt the truth of those words, but he was not done yet.

"Will you do one thing more?"

Aranloth raised an eyebrow. "Perhaps. Ask, and we will see."

Faran glanced at Ferla, and then back toward the lòhren.

"Ferla is in as great a danger as I am. It's even worse for her because she doesn't have to be. She could have walked away, but she hasn't. Will you teach her just as you teach me? She needs it every bit as much as I do."

It was a reasonable thing to ask, and Faran knew it was right to do so. He was not sure what Aranloth's reaction would be though. So far as Faran new, a woman had never before learned the arts of the knights.

Aranloth's reaction was not what he expected though. The old man grew solemn, and he stood from where he sat on the broken wall. Then he bowed to each of them in turn.

"I hold the sacred trust," he said. "I will be Osahka to you, Ferla, and to you, Faran. The mysteries are deep, and the journey long. But I will guide you if you follow."

This seemed like a ceremony, but Faran had no idea what to do or say next. But Kareste whispered in his ear, and he repeated the words she gave him.

"I, Faran, of Dromdruin Village, will walk the path down which you lead me. You are Osahka, and I am Kasellah, the follower who learns."

Kareste looked at Ferla. "Is this what you wish?"

She stood closer, and Faran felt her shoulder brush his own.

"It is."

"Then say the words also."

She did so, and the sound of her voice was grave and intent. It seemed like she swore an oath, and perhaps that was what it was.

"Done!" Aranloth said, and he gave Kareste one of those secret looks they seemed to share.

"Well, old man," she said by way of reply. "Where to now?"

"Now, we go to the one place where we can be sure of quickly finding the weapons and armor that these two most need."

Slowly, Kareste's face paled. "You cannot be serious," she said.

3. The Tombs of the Letharn

Kareste took a step back from the old man. "Now it makes sense why you chose this ring of standing stones."

Aranloth nodded. "Yes, it does."

"It makes sense, but that doesn't mean it isn't too dangerous." She glanced at Faran and Ferla, and then faced the lòhren again. "They're not ready for … such a place."

"Even so, it is necessary."

Kareste looked away, doubt written on her face. And maybe even fear.

Faran wondered what sort of place could provoke that kind of reaction from her.

"Where would you take us?" he asked.

The old man stood. He showed little sign of the ailment that had troubled him before, but with someone like Aranloth, it was hard to tell. He could survive on force of will alone.

"Time to be walking," Aranloth said by way of answer. "I'll think on whether we must go where I plan, or if there's an alternative. Maybe, as we walk, I'll see another way."

That sounded fair enough, and Faran, for his part, would be glad to get away from the standing stones. They had saved him, but he had nearly died within their circle too. Better to put distance between himself and a place like that.

Aranloth led them down the hill. Once, there had been a road here. There still was, of sorts. Time had buckled it, lifting paving stones in some places and dropping them low in others. In some, they lay rent apart as though the earth itself had heaved and scattered them. Rain and sun and ice had done their work too. So had floods and erosion, which in some areas covered the stones with a layer of dirt.

But few were the weeds and patches of grass. Shadows lay everywhere, cast by great buildings that had toppled and yet, ruined as they were, their remnants still stood tall enough to throw shade and stifle growth.

From time to time, rubble blocked the road and the old man led them around it to come back onto it on the other side. Faran did not like the road much, but he liked walking within the ruins of the buildings even less. Here, they might pass through a door that remained standing and into a room that people had lived in long, long before Faran was born, and it made him feel strange. In rooms like those, families had sat and talked. They had feasted and laughed. They had cried at bad news and celebrated good. But they were all dead now.

The whole city stank of death. Not to Faran's nose, but to his mind. He wanted to be away from here and to feel the green, living grass beneath his feet once more. Or to see the branch of a tree move in the breeze. Everything in the ruins was still, and stillness meant death.

Down the long hill Aranloth led them, but the city was far vaster than it looked. The road kept going, and there seemed no end to it. Nor to the buildings on either side. Occasionally, one of these stood relatively undamaged. Some were five stories high, but Faran was sure from the size of some of the piles of rubble that others had been even taller.

The shadows lengthened. A cold wind sprang up from the north, and Aranloth called a halt. It surprised Faran. Perhaps the old man still suffered from whatever ailment the Traveling had brought on, though he looked well enough now.

Faran would have preferred to keep going and leave the city behind. But everyone, not just Aranloth, could do with some rest. And at least here the buildings offered shelter from the wind.

"This will do," the lòhren said.

He led them through a doorway, the wooden door of which had long since succumbed to the weather and all that remained were rusted hinges attached to the stone casing of the frame.

The walls had collapsed too, but a square perimeter remained of its base. This was about five feet high. Tall enough, Faran surmised, to block out the wind. But tall enough also to make a good defense against attackers. Not that Aranloth gave any indication that he was worried about any. It was just wise to be prepared, and Faran approved.

Most of the rubble had fallen outside the walls. But inside there was some, and this they worked quickly to clear out except for some larger stones that would serve as seats.

They ate then, and it was a cold meal for there was no timber at hand in this ancient city to burn. And Aranloth told them of where he intended to go.

"Ordinary weapons and armor will not serve against the things of sorcery that may attack you," he said. "You need things crafted with the skill of the ancient world and imbued with magic of their own."

Kareste shifted uncomfortably on her seat. "Just tell them where you intend to go, old man."

Aranloth went on. "This is the city of the Letharn. Nearby, are their tombs. All the Letharn that ever lived and died are buried there. It is a vast network of caves and tunnels, buried beneath the ground. But it isn't just a burial place. There also are stored the treasures of the nation, and the Letharn empire was immense, and it endured for thousands of years. The wealth in treasures, and objects of esteem, is incalculable."

Kareste looked pointedly at the old man. "And tell them why this wealth is still there after all these years, and why the tombs have never been plundered."

"Because the tombs are guarded," Aranloth answered quietly.

Faran was mindful of Kareste's wariness. Yet curiosity had a hold of him.

"Magic," he said to the old man. "Magic guards the tombs."

Aranloth gave him a sharp look. "You catch on quickly, where magic is concerned. And you're right. Magic of a deadly kind guards them. Perhaps the greatest magic ever invoked. Certainly one of the most dangerous."

The old man did not seem to judge the ancients for their choices. He neither said what they had done was good or bad. But the sense of power, raw and primal, in the magic they had invoked was clear to be heard. He respected them, or at the very least respected their accomplishments.

"This much you have to understand first," Aranloth went on. "The Letharn held strong beliefs. The tombs were sacred to them, not just for reverence of the dead that were interred there but because of the magic of the place itself. They believed it a gateway to another world. They believed it the gateway to an afterlife. It was their custom to be buried there in order to access that gateway. So, no matter where they died, no matter if it was a thousand leagues away, they were brought to the tombs for interment. The greatest punishment of all, handed out to those who committed the wort crimes, was to be buried elsewhere."

Faran thought he understood. "So they protected the tombs with magic as dearly, even more dearly, than they guarded anything in life."

"Exactly so. And they intended that guarding to last for eternity. Great as their empire was, they knew it would not last. Nothing lasts forever, and they would protect their earthly remains, as well as the treasures buried with them that they would use in the afterlife, for as long as the world should endure."

Ferla pulled the hood of her cloak up against the remnants of the cold breeze that still found its way into their enclosure.

"What magic did they invoke, Aranloth? And what is the protection against it? Surely there must be one, otherwise the Letharn could not have entered their own tombs to bury their dead."

Faran was impressed. He had missed that entirely.

"There are two things that they did, and you must be mindful of it every moment we are there," Aranloth said. "The first is this. Most of the treasure you will see is powdered with a deadly poison. It will kill you as surely as a sword stroke. On no account, ever, touch any treasure unless I say that it is safe. Do you agree to that?"

Faran and Ferla both nodded, and the lòhren continued.

"The magic invoked is more dangerous still. It guards the tombs like a dog guards its master's property. It can take any form, and its power is immense. Usually, though, it takes the form of three women. They are known as the three sisters, or the harakgar."

"And how are they defeated?" Ferla asked.

"They cannot be defeated or killed," Aranloth said. "But they can be held off. For this, the ancients wove words of power into the magic that summoned them. These words of power act as a kind of key. Without them, you cannot penetrate far into the tombs without being slain. Without them, you cannot leave again carrying any treasure, no matter that it is nothing more than a copper coin."

Faran thought about all this. He was beginning to see why Kareste was scared.

"Do we really need to go there?" he asked.

"You do if you want weapons and armor to match the training I'll give you. And if you want to be able to face the kind of sorcery that will be sent against you if you are found again."

That was enough for Faran. However dangerous the tombs sounded, facing enemies such as he had without help would be worse. And what if Aranloth or Kareste were not there? He would be killed almost instantly.

Ferla was looking at him, and he thought he saw resolve in her expression. She must have been thinking exactly the same things he was.

"I'll go to the tombs," he said.

"As will I," Ferla added.

Kareste looked away. She made no further argument against it, but it was clear she still thought this a bad idea.

"Then it is settled," Aranloth said. "Tonight, we will rest, and tomorrow we will reach them."

The afternoon sun was dropping low, but there was still some time left before evening. Faran did not look forward to being shut up in this enclosure all night. And he wanted a chance to talk to Ferla as well.

"It's safe here isn't it, in the ruins? I think I might go for a little walk before the night sets in. I get restless in confined spaces like this."

Aranloth hesitated, but then shrugged. "The ruins should be safe. But don't go far. Night isn't long away, and you don't want to be trying to find your way back in the dark."

Faran stood, and he was glad that Ferla did as well. Together, they made their way out of the enclosure and back onto the main road.

There seemed a little more light here outside the enclosure, but dusk was falling. He really did not like this place. They had not reached the tombs yet, but this place seemed like a tomb to him. It was like a vast graveyard, and the relic of each building a gravestone.

They moved down one of the side streets. The hill flattened out here, and the buildings seemed more intact. Many of them stood there, windows and doors gaping in undamaged walls.

"Thank you for including me in Aranloth's training," Ferla said.

"You really do need it as much as I do," he answered. "Aranloth was quick to agree, too. It was almost like I asked for something he had already decided on."

"Perhaps he had. I thought he was quick to agree as well." Then she gave his shoulder a mock punch. "But he probably knows that I'm the better fighter of the two of us."

He grinned back at her. "Not by much. But yes you are."

They walked in companionable silence for a while. But soon the street opened up onto a large square. It was hundreds of feet long and hundreds of feet wide. In the center was some construction, probably a fountain, but neither of them wanted to go so far out in the open. They had left the danger of elù-draks behind, at least for a good while, but habits died hard.

Instead, they walked along the southern perimeter staying close to the cover of the buildings. There was a kind of roofed walkway, and Faran realized that market stalls would have been placed along it and protected from rain and sunlight. There were even pieces of wood here and there, remnants of tables or benches that had survived in this dryer environment. And quite a few wooden doors still hung, if at strange angles, at entrances.

They were halfway along when Ferla looked up and pointed at a window two stories above.

"What's that?"

Faran looked, and just as his gaze fixed on the window he saw a shadowy movement through it, but it was there and gone so fast he could not be sure.

"I don't know," he said. "I thought I saw something. But maybe not."

"There was something there," she replied. "I don't know what either. Perhaps it was only an owl. Maybe."

He kept gazing at the window. "There's only one way to find out."

Ferla was not so sure. "What if it's dangerous?"

"Aranloth said the city should be safe. Neither Lindercroft nor the king could have found us again so quickly. Let's have a look."

Ferla followed behind him, if reluctantly, as he entered the building. On this one, the wooden door had fallen off its hinges and lay across the threshold. At the touch of one of Faran's boots, the timber of its corner disintegrated to dust.

They moved inside. It was quite dark, for part of the tile roof remained intact. It was not a large room, and rubble and debris lay scattered everywhere. Much of it was from tiles that had fallen down, but some was timber.

The timber had come from a stairway against the back wall. Most of it remained intact though, and Faran touched it. It was more solid than the door had been.

"Don't even think about it," Ferla said. "Neither of us is walking up those stairs. They're not safe."

Faran was about to make an argument for why they should, though in truth he knew she was right, when he saw a shadow at the top of the stairs. Again, he caught only a glimpse. But this time it seemed distinctly manlike. Yet just as before, it was gone before he could be certain of anything.

There was a creak above, and Faran saw a sliver of timber fall down. Then the whole ceiling began to move.

"Get out!" he cried. Pushing Ferla ahead of him, they ran for the entrance. They had not reached it when the walls began to move as well, and the grinding sound of brick on brick filled the air with dread.

They leaped and dived through the entrance. Then they raced across the walkway and into the open square beyond. Behind them, the building collapsed with a long boom that rolled through the ruined city and sent a cloud of dust billowing into the air.

They stood in the square, panting and white-faced.

"That was close," Ferla whispered.

"Too close. But the building did not look like it was ready to collapse."

Kareste came into view then, crossing the square toward them. She looked like she had been running, but she was not now.

"You two find trouble wherever you go," she said when she reached them. Despite her light words, there was relief on her face. "What happened?"

Faran told her about the shadow in the window, and how they went to investigate.

"And did you see the shadow when you went inside?"

"I saw something," Faran answered. "I'm not sure what. It looked like a man, but it could not have been. It was there and then it was gone."

"And what of you, Ferla?" Kareste asked.

Ferla drew a long breath. "I saw exactly what Faran saw. But just like him, I can't be sure what it was. It did seem manlike. Maybe we should look in the rubble? If it was a person we have to help."

Kareste shook her head. "There are no people here. No one comes to this long-dead city."

"What caused the shadow then?" Faran asked.

She did not answer him, and that alarmed him. She might have said it was a bird. Or their imagination. But she offered nothing. Instead, she led them back to their camp.

But Faran now knew. There had been a shadow when Aranloth stumbled coming out of the circle of standing stones. There had been a shadow here. And they were both the same, and Kareste suspected it.

And that shadow had lured them into the building and then tried to kill them.

4. Brand of the Duthenor

They passed the night in the enclosure without incident. The cool north wind blew harder, but faded away toward dawn. And they kept a watch at all times.

No one questioned the need for a watch. No one asked what they watched against. It was enough that they all felt a sense of unease, and they all slept better knowing someone was still awake, keeping a lookout for the unexpected.

At first light they ate a swift breakfast and broke camp. Aranloth led them again, winding his way down the long slope and the road that once must have borne the tread of countless boots and the passage of hundreds, if not thousands, of riders and wagons each day.

The size of the ruins astounded Faran. And there were many things to see that caught his interest. Statues lined the way at times, and grand buildings still stood among the rubble. There were parks where trees flourished, and more squares. But all the while they moved downhill and eventually, as they came to flatter lands, they left the city behind.

The road continued, but it was no longer paved. It was a long stretch of grass, barely distinguishable from the grasslands all around. But there were signs here of farms. Cottages still stood in places, but mostly they had fallen. Yet still their foundations showed. Here and there were signs of fences made by hedging. But most of all there were remnants of orchards. Fruit trees grew prolifically, though the original orchards had died out thousands of years ago.

Now that they were in the open, Faran could see a green land spread out below them. It was hemmed in on either side by two rivers, and beyond it rose a long escarpment. From this, the flashing light of a mighty waterfall caught his gaze, even from so far away.

Aranloth set a brisk pace, but he still looked tired. Or maybe just somber. This must once have been his home. He did not say so, but it was clear from the troubled look in his gaze. At least, so Faran thought. But he recalled hearing a legend once that the lòhrens were founded by him, and based on the wizard-priests of the Letharn. And that Aranloth had been one of those.

It seemed likely to him. Aranloth had a look to his eyes that spoke of seeing the vastness of the world over a long time, and much of it bad. Yet for the most part he remained cheerful, which was a feat if he was as old as Faran thought and legend claimed.

Everything was quiet and peaceful, but that did not stop Faran looking behind him from time to time. There was no sign of the shadow. Nor was there any sign of Lindercroft, and both of those were good things.

He hated the feeling of being hunted and pursued. Even now, when there was no reason for it, he still felt it. Or at least worried about it. He should be safe from Lindercroft, but the fear was still with him. Fear cast a shadow. What had happened before sent a specter of itself ahead of him. And to beat that fear, he must face it.

Learning the arts of the knights was the best way to do that. He could prepare himself for what might happen in the future. He and Ferla could learn the skills they needed to stay alive.

Aranloth called a halt to rest and eat lunch. Faran was surprised at how quickly the morning had passed, but the noon sun shone down from above, and he suddenly felt the weariness of a long walk. He would be glad to sit and eat.

But even as he did so he found a patch of grass and faced the others, looking back at the ruins and checking for any sign of movement along their back trail.

Their food stores were getting lower, and they ate frugally to stretch them out. But they did eat well. There was some hardened cheese left, and this they had with some hazelnuts and dried fruit.

They rested a little while after they ate, and while they did so Aranloth drew out a knife from somewhere within his robes and cut a slender branch off a nearby plum tree. The wood was young and whippy, and he whittled away at it quietly while the others talked.

Eventually, Faran asked him what it was.

"A training sword," the lòhren answered. "A primitive one, but it will serve for the moment."

"But we'll need two. I can't spar Ferla unless she has one as well."

The old man looked at him with amusement. "One will suffice. The training methods of the knights are somewhat unique. At least, when I train them."

Faran just shook his head. He had no idea what Aranloth was talking about, but there was no point disputing his methods. Legend claimed he *had* taught the knights not just magic but also martial skill.

"Have you worked out the secrets of the knights yet?" Aranloth asked, finishing what he was doing with the branch.

"It seems like there's quite a few of them," Faran said. "But no, I haven't."

"No matter," Aranloth replied briskly. "You will."

The lòhren stood then and threw the practice sword to Faran. He caught it deftly and swung it in the air a few times to test it.

"It'll do," he said. Actually, it felt surprisingly sword-like in his hands. "But now what? Will you teach me some techniques?"

"No," the lòhren replied. "I want to see what you know already and how good, or bad, you are."

"My grandfather did teach me. I'm not *bad*. It's just that I could be a lot better."

"We'll see. Hold the sword up, and be ready."

"Hold it up for what? I have no one to spar."

"Yes you do. I'll give you one. The image you see will seem real. Blows will hurt. The shock of a strike will travel down your arm. But it is illusion."

Suddenly an image appeared before Faran. A red-bearded man, not very tall but sturdily built, came rushing at him and slashed wildly with a wooden practice sword of his own.

Even though caught by surprise, Faran stepped neatly to the side, avoided the blow and thrust his own blade up into the man's abdomen.

The red-bearded man disappeared with a flash of light, and Faran grinned.

"I told you I wasn't bad. This is easy."

"Well it should be," Aranloth said. "That man was a farmer who only held a sword once in his life, and he died wielding it. He had courage, but not any skill."

Faran was surprised. "You mean he was real?"

"Not what you saw. That was just illusion drawn from my mind of how he fought. That's how the magic works. It takes my memories and makes them seem real."

"Well, how about a worthy opponent then?"

The lòhren gave him a cool look. "You have much to learn. That man was worthy, he just had no skill with a blade. Here is one who will test you more."

Another image appeared. It was of a larger man, yet he stood with a casual grace that spoke of the warrior. A sword was in his hand, its blade bright. On his head was a helm, gleaming silver. He was no knight, but he reminded Faran of both Lindercroft and the king. Only he seemed nobler than they, kinglier by far than even the king had seemed.

Kareste hissed between her teeth, but Faran did not look at her. He could not take his gaze off the image before him. The eyes of the warrior were blue, and they were cold as ice. Not because he was heartless, but because when he held a sword in his hand it was to kill. There was implacable determination in them that Faran had never seen before. Nor did he even see the blow that crashed into his head.

His opponent had barely seemed to move, but Faran reeled back, feeling the knock to his head, but only faintly. Those blue eyes regarded him once more, and Faran trembled. This man was death to face in combat. Then the image slowly faded away.

"That was no farmer," Faran said, and his voice shook.

He expected Aranloth to answer, but it was Kareste who replied.

"That was Brand of the Duthenor," she told him. "And you are not ready to face the likes of him. Even Lindercroft would quail before one such as that."

Brand. Faran had heard stories of him. Who had not? No wonder that he had been beaten so easily.

"Give the sword to Ferla," Aranloth said. "Let's see what she can do."

Ferla took the sword from him and turned to face the lòhren. She held the blade steady before her, standing poised and relaxed. When the image of the red-bearded man appeared, she did not wait for him to attack but gracefully stepped forward and ran him through even as he lifted his own blade.

The image disappeared in a flash of light again, and Aranloth clapped.

"Well done! Attack can be the best form of defense."

They continued their journey then, and the land around them changed. Aranloth seemed to know exactly where he was going, and he led them through patches of trees and into lower country. Faran heard the rush of water nearby, and he knew he was close to one of the rivers he had seen earlier. Ahead, the land rose into the massive escarpment which he had also seen.

There was little vegetation on the face of the escarpment. Here and there were a few stumpy bushes, but for the most part there were only steep buttresses of dark stone.

They drew closer, and the roar of the waterfall that he had seen earlier became loud, and then as Faran emerged from a small wood he saw it spilling down a quarter mile stretch of rock. He had never seen anything like it, and the roar grew deafening as they came closer.

Beneath the falls lay a lake, but it was no placid body of water. It was a churning maelstrom, and from here two rivers sprang and ran to separate courses, forming an ever-expanding angle between them. The hill behind Faran, on which the ruins slowly crumbled, was the center of that angle, and the heart of the Letharn empire of old.

The falls thundered in his ears. Water sprays filled the air, cleared, and then became thicker again.

"Follow me!" Aranloth bellowed above the tumult, and he led them a little to the right. They crossed an ancient bridge over to a small island, and then another to their right again.

The stone of the bridges was pitted by age, and slick beneath their boots. But they crossed quickly. The rivers lay to their left now, and before them a gorge opened up and ran toward the top of the escarpment. It was hard to see because of all the water spray, but they moved up it and the air swiftly cleared and the roar of the falls lessened.

The gorge widened as it ascended, and a ledge was cut into the cliff on the left. This Aranloth led them onto, and they followed him upward as the path rose over the ever-increasing drop to the right.

"One at a time only," Aranloth called over his shoulder. "And be careful of your footing."

Faran did not like it. The ledge was narrow, and though he hugged close to the cliff, the chasm seemed like a yawning mouth to his right willing him to fall into it.

He tried not to look anywhere but the rocky path ahead of him, but the cliff on the other side of the ravine drew his attention. There, great figures were carved into the stone, and they became taller and grander as the ledge he climbed ascended higher.

The figures were now hundreds of feet tall. Countless years had aged them. Wind and water had attacked them. The ravages of time wore away at them, yet they still remained images of awe.

Farmers there were, scythes in hand or guiding ploughs drawn by oxen. Hunters were shown, and their quarry. Weavers and potters and warriors there were too. The warriors looked grim, and they wore fine armor. Almost Faran felt that they were watching him, judging him, and staying their hand to attack. For now.

And higher there were priests. Solemn figures. Wise. Their pitted eyes gazing out at the world with the sad gaze of the philosopher.

But last came figures that must be royalty. They wore no crowns nor sat on thrones. But they were kings and queens. Or emperors and empresses. Diadems were on their brows, and the art of the carvers made it seem that the stones caught light and cast it out over the chasm.

Faran felt the weight of time. More, he felt the weight of destiny. Would he make something of himself? Would he be worthy one day to have a statue carved of him? Would his likeness be remembered after death consigned him to the oblivion of the great dark?

He glanced back at the way they had come. Far away he saw the great hill on which the ruins of the vast city of the Letharn sprawled. Tallach-far Aranloth had called it. But Faran wondered how many in all the world still knew that name.

The thunder of the great falls had receded to a murmur. Faran looked ahead again, and they came now to a place that showed signs of damage. The ledge had been repaired here, perhaps from a landslide. Looking at the cliff above it, it seemed that the rock face was less weathered. But there were char marks as well on the stone, and he surmised that magic had been involved. Some battle had been fought on this spot.

Just after this, the ledge altered. It cut farther into the cliff-face forming a recess. Beyond, the ledge narrowed again and continued its way up to the top of the escarpment. But it was the recess that Aranloth was interested in, and Faran saw why.

It was not a large space, but Faran was glad of the extra room and moved away from the chasm that unnerved him.

In the center of the recess stood a stele. It was a strange looking thing, and there was writing on it. The script was like nothing Faran had ever seen, and must have been the language of the Letharn. But Aranloth did not translate it, and Faran did not ask. He was not sure he wanted to know.

It was the cave that attracted Faran's attention though. But he soon realized it was no cave but a man-made tunnel. Here was the entrance to the tombs.

"Do not enter without me," Aranloth warned. "Or you will die. Now is no time to enter anyway. We'll wait until dawn."

Faran looked out over the chasm. It was swallowed by shadows, and the light had that feel to it of late afternoon. Perhaps it was not the time to enter the tombs, but it would be a long, long night out here on the ledge.

5. The Shadow of Fear

They settled down for the night. It was yet another fireless camp, for there was no timber here.

Faran felt exposed on the recess. Should an elù-drak find them, they would be vulnerable. But Aranloth did not seem concerned by the possibility. That, at least, was comforting. Finally, Faran had left his enemies behind him. It might be months, even years before they found him again.

Unless he found them first. The king and Lindercroft had ordered the destruction of his village and the murder of innocent people. For that, they must be brought to justice.

But these were thoughts of the future. Just now, he wanted to know of the past.

"Tell me more of the Letharn?" he asked Aranloth.

They sat quietly in a small group. They had eaten, and the sun had set. The ledge above them and below them was lost in shadows. The massive carved figures gazed invisibly across the chasm. The entrance to the tombs was close, but it was even darker than the night which filled the ravine like a river.

"The Letharn," Aranloth began, "were the greatest of people. And the worst. Their knowledge surpassed any nation that has come after them. Take your pick. Healing, farming, smithcraft, magic, mining, embalming, chariot building, book binding. It doesn't matter. In almost any field they had the greatest skill. But with that went pride."

The old man gazed out into the night. There was nothing to see, but Faran did not think he was looking at the present.

"You were one of them, weren't you?"

The old man sighed. "I was one of them. I knew their glory before they fell. I still atone for their sins."

Faran felt an inkling then of the weight of years this old man carried, burdened by emotions that someone as young as himself would struggle to understand. And he understood something else, too.

Aranloth was driven to do the things he did. He was a figure of legend, standing against the dark things of the world. He risked his life for the great and the small alike. He did it because that was who he was, but also to make up for something his people had done. Maybe that he had been a part of himself. How great a sin must it have been if he still atoned for it after all this time?

"Why did they fall?" he asked.

"That is like asking why the sun rises, lad. Some things just are." The old man considered him a moment, and then went on as though deciding that for once he would give a detailed answer. "Consider this part of your training. Nothing lasts forever. Nothing. Even this earth upon which we walk will one day burn in fire and spin away as a cold rock into the void. The sun itself shall snuff out, and all that you see now in the starry sky likewise. One day. But not today. The death of people is quicker. But nations, just like people, die also. The Letharn had their day. They did much good, but they spawned great evil also. And they got worse as they aged. Not all the gold in Alithoras was enough to glut their greed. In the end, their demise was a good thing."

It was a lot to take in, but Faran thought he understood. Nations could indeed die just like people.

"Is that what's happening now to Faladir? Is the realm dying."

Aranloth raised an eyebrow. "You have your grandfather's swift grasp of situations. Yes, Faladir is dying. But all nations know periods of ebb and flow. Sometimes they rise again from their defeats. It may be so with Faladir. The seventh knight might bring renewal."

"It will not be me."

"Perhaps not. It may be another. We will see. But this much has been your lesson. Nothing lasts forever, and even the great forces of the cosmos fade. The better you can read these changes, in the large and the small alike, the better you can judge when to act, and how. And maybe, just as a nation in jeopardy can find renewed vigor, so too might you."

Faran nodded. "This is why you wouldn't let me fight Lindercroft. His power is great, and mine is nothing. But in time, I may learn enough to rival him?"

"Exactly," Aranloth said appreciatively. "You really do grasp these things quickly."

Ferla leaned forward. "But the knights have greater skill than us. How can we hope to ever match them, unless we wait until they reach their dotage?"

Aranloth grinned. "A fair point. But I am Osahka. I will guide you, and I will give of my knowledge. And I will train you as even the knights never were."

The night had worn on about them, and they slept soon after. They took turns to keep watch, but it was hard to see anything in the darkness that engulfed the recess. Even the stele, which they were close to, was but a dim shadow.

Faran slept. His would be the last watch of the night, and Kareste would wake him when her turn was done.

Dreams troubled his sleep. They came and went, but ever there was a fear in them. Few he remembered when he came to wakefulness, but sleep, and more dreams, pulled him under again and he tossed restlessly.

This also gave him fear. In the dark, it was easy to imagine that the edge of the recess was much closer, and that he might tumble off in his sleep to fall and crash against the jagged rocks far below.

He was deeply asleep when the worst dream came. The stele, not far from him, twisted to look where he lay. Faran wanted to scream, but he could not. And the stele, after surveying him, detached itself from the earth and crept toward him. It was a man now, or the shadow of a man, and terror ran before it like wind before a storm.

Long hands reached for his neck, and Faran struggled. He thrashed and punched and then rose out of sleep like a man rushing up to the surface of a lake where he had been drowning.

It was dark. Aranloth and Ferla were nearby, sleeping. The stele was where it always had been, and it was still. Leaning against it was Kareste. She was awake, and he saw that her head was turned in his direction. He must have made a noise or moved during his nightmare.

And it *had* been a nightmare, but the feel of it was not receding. Rather, it grew stronger.

He saw then something beyond Kareste. It was a shadow, darker even than the other shadows, and it stepped. It was no dream this time, but real. And though it did not move again it had given itself away.

"Awake!" cried Faran.

At the same moment, Kareste must have sensed something also for her head spun back so that she could see back down the ledge up which they had climbed yesterday.

"Enemy in the camp!" she yelled, and bright light burst from the tip of her staff.

The light was blinding, and Faran half shielded his eyes. For a moment, he saw nothing, but then he saw the shadow again, and the light had not dispelled it.

Tall the shadow stood, manlike, and even in discovery it did not flee as it had done before. For Faran knew it now. It was the same shadow he had seen in the ring of standing stones and later in the ruined building.

Kareste leaped up, and shadows danced all over the recess in the flaring light of her staff. But the intruder did not retreat. She sent lòhren-fire darting at it, but it dodged and came at her.

Leaping to his feet, Faran drew a knife and sent it hurtling through the dark. He was not sure if he missed his target, or if the knife just passed through it, but he saw the blade gleam as it tumbled away into the chasm.

Ferla did not throw a knife, but she held one in her hand and joined Kareste. Faran followed a moment later, and even as the shadow swung back and forth to look at them all, more lòhren-fire flared. This time it came from Aranloth.

The shadow dodged again, and then it bounded down the ledge and disappeared in the dark. Kareste sent a blast of magic after it, but it merely roared against rock and stone and then sputtered away into the dark again. Of their enemy, there was no sign.

"What *is* that thing?" Ferla asked.

"I don't know what it is," Aranloth replied. "But it hunts us."

The old man looked tired again, as though the battle had taxed him greatly. But Faran had seen him do far more and look less tired than that.

"Whatever it is," Kareste added, "it's getting stronger and bolder."

That was something that Faran had not thought of, but it was true. It was getting a more definite shape as well. It was no longer just a vague shadow, but distinctly manlike.

They moved back on the recess and farther away from the ledge, sitting down once more. But Kareste did not let the light of her staff out, and they watched the ledge closely. There would be no more sleep for any of them now, but dawn was not that far away.

Faran studied Aranloth as he sat, still holding his staff upright in his hands.

"You really don't know what it is?"

The old man slowly shook his head. "I wish that I did."

"Can you not even guess?"

"Guessing is a dangerous game. But this much I think is right. Whatever it is, it wishes us no good. It has tried to kill, and there is no reason to think it won't again."

It was not what Faran wanted to hear. "You said that Lindercroft and the king would not be able to follow us when we Traveled. But it seems that one of them still managed to send something after us."

It was Kareste who answered him. "As Aranloth said, guessing is a dangerous game. But he and I have talked about this. Our enemies in Faladir don't have the knowledge for this. They don't know how the standing stones work. Whatever that shadow thing is, and whatever its purpose, it has nothing to do with them."

Aranloth twisted his staff idly in his hands, but his gaze was sharp when he looked at Faran.

"Many things are in doubt, but this much is true. Whatever the thing is, it will not survive where we go next. Nothing enters or leaves the tombs unless it knows the words of power that stave off the harakgar. Nothing."

"And yet," Kareste said, "it will still follow us. There's a determination to its actions."

"Then it must surely die," Aranloth answered.

As they sat on the recess and talked, the sky grew gray and the night faded away. They ate a meagre meal, and then Aranloth stood.

"The tombs await," he said. "The sooner we enter them and retrieve the weapons and armor, the sooner we can leave them."

They followed him inside, but Faran could not help a quick glance behind him to see if the shadow was anywhere in sight.

6. Your Time Will Come

It was dark in the cave, and the smell of death was strong. But worse to Faran was the sense of a presence. It whispered in the back of his mind, and it was hostile to anything that lived.

He knew what that presence was. The harakgar of which Aranloth warned. The lòhren had said how powerful they were, but the force of their enmity and the strength of the magic struck like a blow, and though warned, Faran was ill-prepared.

Yet when he glanced at Ferla, he saw that she showed nothing more than wariness. Aranloth and Kareste were not likely to show any fear. They were too powerful themselves, and too schooled in the art of hiding their emotions. But why should he feel the strength of the enmity more than Ferla?

It was not long before they came across the first bodies. These were revealed by the light at the tips of the lòhrens' staffs. But they had not been laid to rest here in some sort of funeral.

The bodies lay scattered over the floor. They had died entering the tombs, and likely enough they were robbers of some sort. But it was proof, if any were needed, that this place was guarded.

Swords lay on the floor, out of their sheathes. These men had fought, or at least tried to. But it must have been long ago. What remained of them now was the dry husk of their bodies, withered by time, but still intact. Though it was a cave, no scavengers had ever entered here to disturb the corpses. More confirmation, in its way, of the power of the harakgar.

They moved ahead, the steady light of the lòhrens showing the way. And the tunnel changed swiftly, going into a steep decline.

Faran felt the whispering presence in this place grow stronger. He had the feeling that the harakgar had been far away in the tombs, but they were here now. Distance meant nothing to them. There was little restraint on the magic, and he knew that in this place, they ruled.

He had not seen them yet. But he knew he would soon. They were close. Watching. Thinking. He looked for them, but saw nothing. Yet Aranloth sensed them also, as surely he must have better than Faran could. He held his staff a little higher, and he seemed ready and poised.

There was a sense of movement in the air, and the lights dimmed a little then flared brighter. Dread hung over the travelers, the intruders into a realm that was not theirs. Here, the harakgar held dominion, and they finally showed themselves.

There were three of them. And like sisters they appeared. Long was their hair, and it twined around their naked bodies. Their eyes were bright, but their gaze held no human emotion.

In their hands were long knives, sickle shaped and serrated. These they lifted and glided toward Aranloth.

The lòhren stood his ground. If he were worried, he gave no sign of it. Instead, he lifted his staff higher still, and his voice rang out in this hollow place deep within the earth.

"Har nere ferork. Skigg gar see!"

It was the charm. These were the words of power. This was the one weakness woven into the great magic that had summoned the harakgar. And even like a key turning in a lock, Faran felt something change.

The harakgar ceased to move toward them. But their eyes flashed hatred. The charm held them, but if they had their way they would rend flesh and shred minds.

The three figures flowed and melded into one another, moving like a sinister mist. As one they raised their serrated knives, and then these fell to the floor with the clang of steel. But when Faran looked, there was no sign of the weapons. It was meant as a warning rather than a submission to authority. The message was a challenge. Proceed if you dare, but we will watch and wait. We will appear again, and test you.

With a screech of rending stone, the mist that was the harakgar passed into the ceiling above and disappeared.

Aranloth stepped ahead again, his tread steady. He did not even look at the ceiling as he passed below where the harakgar had exited, but Faran did. And despite the noise, the stone was undamaged.

The tombs started now. Within the walls to each side were alcoves. Some small, and some larger. There were side passages also, though these were narrow. But all contained the remains of humans. Bones gleamed in the light, and skulls, toppled at strange angles, leered.

Sometimes the remains had not decomposed. They had been embalmed, and withered flesh clung to the bones.

"Touch nothing!" Aranloth reminded them all.

Faran could not see any sign of poison, and he wondered what poison could endure through the long years. But he did not doubt Aranloth's word.

Nor did he understand the need for protection against theft. There seemed nothing here that anyone would want to steal. Mostly, each alcove contained nothing more than a body. Although sometimes there were tools such as chisels, hammers and pottery wheels. They must have been the tools the dead used in life.

There were bows and arrows too. It was these that Faran most wanted to look at, for they were far different from the ones used in Faladir. But he caught Ferla frowning at him, and ignored them after that. Curious as he was, no bow was worth dying for.

But the tombs soon changed. The artifacts of the poor gave way to the artefacts of the rich. The alcoves were larger, and in them were chariots, some ceremonial with gold-rimmed wheels. There were piles of coins too. Silver and gold. And the dead here were no mere bones or withered remains. They were embalmed and protected against the ravages of time. Gold rings still fitted to fingers whose flesh had not withered. And silver earrings adorned faces that were dead, yet still held the likeness of the living.

Faran shuddered. He did not like the feeling that the dead were watching him, and he sensed the whispering of the harakgar as well. They were behind somewhere, preoccupied now but he knew they would return. They would challenge Aranloth's charm again.

Ahead, the path they followed leveled out. The very rock cracked, like mud at the bottom of a pond that had dried out, and over a fissure a slim bridge leaped to the other side. It was arched, and graceful, and out of place in this grim darkness lit only briefly by the passage of the two lòhrens.

They drew closer. Ahead of the bridge was another stele. It was of black stone, and inlaid with gold was more of the strange script of the Letharn.

Aranloth did not translate it. Nor did Faran ask. Some things might be better not to know.

The sound of rushing water came from somewhere far below. But Faran could not see it.

They stepped onto the bridge and began to cross. Below, where the water should have been, was a dark void. No bottom to the fissure was visible. Yet within that black void, strange lights danced. They moved and ebbed to a graceful rhythm. What they were, Faran could not even begin to guess.

But he did not look down again. Instead, he followed Aranloth as the lòhren strode across quickly. When the old man reached the other side, he turned and waited for the others.

Faran joined him, and turned around also. For a moment, he thought he saw some movement in the shadows beyond the other side of the bridge, but he was not sure. Yet he did see the harakgar.

They sped through the air on wings of fire, streaking toward the group.

Ferla and Kareste ran the last little way and left the bridge. Even as they did so, the voice of Aranloth boomed out.

"*Har nere ferork. Skigg gar see!*"

The harakgar drew up, hovering above the bridge, and their flesh writhed as though on fire and they spat sparks. Angry was the glare of their eyes, and each gaze was like a dagger of hatred and resentment.

Again, Aranloth voiced the charm. "*Har nere ferork. Skigg gar see!*"

The harakgar beat their wings of flame, and then dissolved into smoke that drifted away into the shadows and was lost from sight.

"They seem angry," Kareste said nonchalantly.

Aranloth looked grim. "They're always angry." But he seemed to consider her words more and then spoke again. "But you are right. They are worse than usual."

Faran wondered just how many times Aranloth had been here, and for what purposes. But Aranloth seemed to give the matter no more heed. He turned and led them forward again, but not very far.

Before them was a crossroads. The main way they had been following continued straight ahead, but there were also now smaller tunnels to the left and the right.

Aranloth did not hesitate. "This way," he said, and he took the right tunnel.

This descended also, but not so steeply as before. The alcoves became larger too. They were chambers now, large and supplied with all the household items the dead must have used while alive. The dead were there as well, reposed on beds of stone as if in their houses of long ago that now, in the world above, were nothing more than ruins.

Faran could not judge time down here in this strange place of fear and peace. It seemed they had been walking for a long while, but Aranloth had not called for a rest break and no one seemed tired anyway. Perhaps it would be better to keep walking. The sooner they left here the better.

He kept looking behind him as they walked. He noticed Kareste, coming up the rear as she always did, was doing the same thing. But was she looking for the harakgar, or the shadow that pursued them? And what was he looking for himself?

Aranloth seemed certain that the shadow could not follow them. But the old man had not quite been himself since the circle of standing stones. He could be wrong. And there had been *something* back at the bridge. Perhaps Kareste had seen that also.

They had not traveled much farther when Aranloth's pace began to slow, and then he came to a standstill.

"Beware," the old man said, turning to them, and then he faced the front again.

They gathered close to him, but what instinct warned him of something, Faran did not know. He sensed nothing different here than he had before.

But soon he saw a figure, faint but shining with an inner light, walk toward them. Graceful was that walk, and though slow it spoke of surety and authority.

"The sprits of the dead sometimes walk in this place," Aranloth whispered to them. "There is no danger, but do not anger she who comes. Her power, even in death, is great."

The figure approached. It was a woman, and she seemed neither young nor old. The robes she wore shimmered palely, for they were made of light. As was her figure. There was no substance to her, and yet she seemed real. Certainly, the sharp gaze of her bright blue eyes was real.

A silver diadem was on her head, and it gleamed in the shadowy light. Faran was not sure, but he thought she was an empress, or at least of royal blood. She had that look about her, and she bore also a likeness to the great figures carved on the cliff face opposite the entrance to the tombs.

Aranloth did something Faran had never seen before. He bowed. Not just a slight gesture, but a full-bodied bow of deep respect.

The empress, if empress she was, regarded Aranloth with a cool gaze.

"You yet live," she said, and her voice was a whisper in the air, less solid even than her figure. But she still maintained a tone of authority.

"My work is not yet complete," Aranloth answered. "There is no rest for me, yet."

"Some would say that your work was complete, and cursed, long, long ago."

There was a pause. "Are you one of them, O Queen?"

Some light of the lòhren's staff caught the diadem on her head, and silver flashed in the dark. It made her face seem younger.

"I am not one of them. I judge your deeds fair, and history has proven you correct. Yet still there are whispers among the dead that you betrayed us. They will not cease, but this you know."

"It is not possible to please all people, O Queen, as you know. To some, I am a traitor. To others, a hero. But when the great dark calls me, I shall sleep in peace."

The queen regarded him several long moments. "That is all a man, or a woman, can hope for. Queen or pauper alike. But I do not walk these dark tunnels to speak of the past."

Aranloth straightened, and if he usually looked like an old man, he looked fierce and ready now as a warrior before battle. Age dropped off him like a cloak, and Faran realized it was a guise. Here was the true Aranloth. And he was a figure of power. He seemed ready for any news the queen might offer, and eager for it, though he guessed it might be bad. But knowledge was power, and he was ready to act on whatever he learned.

The queen, for all that she was shorter than Aranloth, seemed to look down upon him.

"You are in grave danger. Take heed! Dark things stir, and forces from the void have been loosed upon the world. But your greatest threat is yourself. You are your own enemy. To prevail, you must become one with yourself."

Faran could make no sense of those words. Legend said that the dead knew the future, but it also said that they spoke in riddles. At least one of those was now proven true.

But the queen was not done. She turned next to Ferla, and regarded her solemnly.

"Your name is written in the stars, girl. You are the quiet one whose name will soon echo across the land, and rumor of it passes even through the void. Be brave, and learn what you must in preparation for your task ahead."

Ferla paled, but she seemed to have no trouble meeting the other's gaze.

"And what will my task be, O Queen?"

"That, you already know. It is not one of your asking, or even to your liking. But you know your duty."

Next, the queen turned to Faran, and her cool gaze rested on him. He saw the eyes of a woman dead long before a time that he considered legend. Yet there was life in them, and for all her remoteness he sensed a kinship with her. She had endured hardships while she lived, and injustice that she longed to right. He sensed it more clearly than any words she could speak, and he wondered about himself that instinct could tell him such a thing, and that he believed it instead of calling it fancy. He had changed since leaving Dromdruin.

"You are not who you think you are," the queen said to him. "The land calls to you, and you have seen the Lady. A strange thing for one so young, when others live lifetimes without seeing her. But you will be one of her great servants, as have some of your ancestors in ages past. You will have burdens to carry, heavier than normal men. But that is fitting, for you are *not* as others. The blood in your veins makes it so."

Faran's mind whirled. He understood nothing of what she said, but she stepped lightly away from him before he could speak.

The queen stood before Kareste. "Your troubled youth is over, and you made wise choices, in the end. Now your service to the land truly begins. And it is needed."

The queen moved again to stand before Aranloth, and she seemed weary now.

"The long sleep calls me again. Beware! Things are not as they seem."

Aranloth made to speak to her again. "O Queen … " But his voice trailed away for she faded from sight and was gone. Strangely, the tombs felt empty without her.

"Who was *she*?" asked Faran.

"The first queen of the Letharn."

Ferla frowned. "But I thought the Letharn were an empire. Does that not make her an empress?"

"The Letharn founded an empire," Aranloth told her. "But they did not start as one. Once, their rule extended only between the two rivers and up to the great hill where the city was later built. She was the queen who began the expansion of the realm. But she did not live to see it grow into an empire."

With that, the lòhren turned to face the front again and began to walk.

"Time presses," he called over his shoulder. "We don't want to spend a moment more in this place than we must."

They moved ahead, and Faran thought on things as they shuffled through the darkness. Only the little pool of lòhren light that surrounded them made this place bearable. Better to focus inward and think than to look out and see the endless dead.

But the words of the queen were just as dark as the tombs, and he could make nothing of them. Not of what she had said about him, nor the others. But he did glance at Ferla from time to time, and he felt proud. If the queen were to be believed, his friend was destined for greatness.

The tunnel turned and dipped, and they came to another bridge like the last. They crossed over quickly, and as before Faran saw no bottom to the fissure below. Only a void of darkness filled by those strange twinkling lights that moved and swayed.

When they had reached the other side Aranloth's face paled. He looked back the way they had come, and his voice was filled with dread when he spoke.

"*It cannot be.*"

But it was, and they all saw it. The shadow that hunted them stood on the far side of the bridge. It was featureless, but without doubt a man.

"Nothing survives in here without the charm," Aranloth said. "Flee! I'll hold the bridge, and catch up to you when the thing is dead."

But the shadow did not seem scared of him, and it stepped onto the bridge and strode forward.

7. Aranloth the White

The shadow strode across the bridge. Manlike it was, yet a thing of shadow also, and fear ran before it like wind before a storm. No attack of stealth was this, but the strike of one who expected to win.

"Move!" shouted Kareste, and she ushered Faran and Ferla forward along the tunnel.

Faran needed no more urging. Fear gripped him, and he ran. But even as he did so, he slowed. Aranloth had befriended him and suffered risk and threat of death on his behalf. He should not be abandoned now.

Even as he thought that, he saw Ferla stop and string her bow. She had thought the same as he.

"Fools!" cried Kareste. "What help could you give Aranloth against such as that?"

But she had stopped herself, and they turned and watched from safety to see what unfolded. Not that they would be safe for long if Aranloth fell.

Kareste stood before them, staff blazing with light. Faran knew that if Aranloth fell, she would be their last hope. But the old man would not fall. He *must* not fall.

The shadow came to the middle of the bridge, and there it paused, suddenly wary. For Aranloth had not run from it, but rather stepped onto the bridge to meet it.

But the shadow, if now cautious, still attacked. It raised its two arms, and crimson fire dripped from its fingertips. Then it thrust them forward and the red fire spurted, leaping from its fingers like a hail of arrows sped from a line of bowmen.

Aranloth raised his staff. His movement was unhurried, but swift as light a shield of silver bloomed before him.

The crimson flame streaked away from the shield and jagged upward to the ceiling. Showers of rock fell down, but Aranloth ignored that and lòhren-fire, silver-white, leaped from his staff at the shadowy form in the middle of the bridge.

Aranloth's opponent raised his arms in a crisscross fashion, and a wall of shadow appeared. It did not block the lòhren-fire, but absorbed it like sand absorbing rain.

Faran held his breath. These two opponents seemed equally matched, and the forces they unleashed amazed him.

But no battle could last forever. There was no such thing as an equal match. One or the other must soon prove to have the greater skill, or at least the greater luck.

Aranloth lifted high his staff. The shadowy figure raced toward him, seeking to close the gap. But a sudden wind blew, driving from Aranloth's staff, and the shadow-figure rolled and tumbled backward. Nearly it fell off the bridge into the chasm below, but on the very precipice it regained its footing and stood defiantly.

It raised its arms, but Aranloth acted first. He retreated, leaping back nimbly across the bridge and spinning a shield of light behind him. A bolt of crimson lightning struck it, and thunder rolled through the tombs.

Faran felt the tremor of it in the stone beneath his boots, and rocks fell once more from the ceiling. The shadow began to advance again, but paused as once more Aranloth raised his staff.

This time, nothing happened. The shadow began to move again, but even as it did the lights that ebbed and flowed in the chasm came suddenly into view. Like a swarm of insects they rose, but they did not attack

Aranloth's enemy. Instead, they clustered all over the bridge itself.

Those small lights kept gathering. There were more of them than stars in the sky, and they piled atop the center of the bridge. They flashed and twinkled, and the light coming from them soon shone brighter than the sun.

Aranloth wheeled back, but he stumbled and fell to his knees. Kareste shouted, and raced forward toward him. And the shadow advanced.

But then the shadow paused again. A moment it stood there as if in thought, and then it too wheeled and ran. Even as it did so, the lights flared, and the span of stone that was the bridge groaned. With a crack like thunder, the center of the bridge snapped, and it slowly bent and toppled into the void. The length of the bridge behind and ahead groaned as well, then it too slipped away into darkness.

Silence fell. Aranloth scrambled on loose rock slipping into the dark where the bridge had uprooted from its joining to the floor of the tunnel. But Kareste reached him in a flurry of robes, and dropping her staff she slid to the ground and grabbed hold of him.

Kareste heaved the old man free of the rubble, and then snatched up her staff again. She gazed across the chasm, but Faran did not think she saw anything more than he did. The shadow was gone, either into the void or back up the tunnel behind.

The strange lights rose and swirled, and then they drifted downward again into the fissure and disappeared from sight.

It took Faran a while to realize that no noise had come up from the chasm. There should have been the smashing sound of stone as the broken bridge hit the bottom. But there was nothing, and that disturbed him. Surely there was a bottom, but that it was so far away that even the sound of a fallen bridge would not reach back up to the surface was disturbing. Next time he crossed one of those, he would *not* look down.

He and Ferla went over to the two lòhrens. Kareste was examining Aranloth for injuries.

"I think your arm is broken, old man," she said.

"It wouldn't be the first time," he answered.

Kareste turned to Ferla. "Get me some cloth. I need long strips." Then she looked at Faran. "I'll need the practice sword Aranloth made."

Kareste worked quickly. She broke the sword in half and trimmed it with a knife. Then she used the cloth Ferla had gathered to bind Aranloth's arm with a splint. Finally, she fashioned a sling for him and handed him back his staff.

"Good as new," she said.

But Aranloth looked far from well. His face was gray, a gash bled from his forehead and his hands trembled. If he felt pain, he hid it well. But he could not hide his sudden frailty. He looked in truth the old man that he was. And that scared Faran.

They allowed him to rest a little while longer, but it was clear that he was lucky to even be able to walk. Kareste took over responsibility for the chant that warded them from the harakgar, and she had to voice it before they set off again, for the harakgar reappeared.

But set off they did, this time with Kareste in the lead and Faran with his arm around the old man to keep him steady. No light came from his staff, and Ferla guarded the rear with her bow strung and an arrow notched.

Aranloth walked with Faran's support, and also by using his staff as a walking stick.

"Let me know if you need rest," Faran said.

Aranloth looked ahead. His gaze determined. "I'll get by. Don't worry about me."

"But I do worry about you. And I worry that thing, whatever it is, isn't dead."

Aranloth looked troubled. "It may not be. I underestimated it."

Faran kept his gaze ahead also, making sure there was nothing on the ground they might trip over. If the old man fell, he might not be able to get up again.

"I thought you said nothing could survive in here without the charm?"

Aranloth shook his head. "I said that, and it's *right*. But before you ask me anything else, let me say I just don't know. I don't know how the shadow lived, and I don't know what it wants, either. Somehow, I'm wrong despite being right."

Faran did not say anything else. He did not want to upset the old man, but it seemed clear what the shadow wanted. It wanted to kill them all, and maybe especially Aranloth. There was something intensely personal about that battle on the bridge.

None of this sounded like anything that Faran had a chance of understanding. It was clear that even the two lòhrens did not know what was happening. It was not, as it sometimes was, that they held knowledge back. It was that they just did not have it in the first place. And it was disturbing to hear that Aranloth, *Aranloth the White,* about whom a thousand legends spoke with a sense of awe for his courage and wisdom, had been wrong.

Faran helped the old man along. Both that, and his being wrong made him seem very human. But that was a two-edged sword. He became suddenly more approachable and less of a forbidding figure. But just now, of all times, they needed the legend.

They moved ahead, shuffling through the darkness, and the light of one lòhren staff alone seemed hardly enough to keep back the dark that pressed in like water filling a bucket.

And worse, Aranloth seemed to be growing weaker.

8. Armor, Swords and Treasure

Kareste led them now, and several times the harakgar had appeared. She repelled them each time with the charm, but it seemed to Faran that they were not repelled as much. There was more to the charm than the mere words alone.

Down they went, deep beneath the earth. Nor was there a path back the way that they had come. The bridge was thrown down. Aranloth was weak, or ill. If Kareste were injured or killed, he and Ferla would die down here in the gloom. They would never find a way out by themselves. They would stay down here forever, two more dead bodies among the millions of those who had gone before.

Faran gritted his teeth and trudged on. No more did he look in the alcoves and the passages filled with the dead. He had seen more of that than he wanted to, and the sight taunted him. *You will be one of us.* That was what he thought he heard the dead say. *Sooner than you think.*

Faran ignored the dead. And he ignored the whisperings in his head. He was young. He was alive, and he had a task to achieve in the world of the living. A task that he *must* achieve.

The tunnels did not change much. Some were wider. Some narrower. There were crossroads at times, and even stairs cut into the stone at places. It was clear though that Kareste knew where they were going. She must have known the tombs, and Aranloth must have told her what their destination was.

Certainly the old man was no help to her now, and he offered no guidance. It was all he could do to put one foot ahead of the other and continue forward. But he did seem just a little stronger.

As they went ahead, they reached a point where the tunnel widened. There were pillars in the center now, and these were carved with scenes of war and battle. The alcoves of the dead disappeared. Instead, great chambers opened up to each side, and these were piled high with gems and jewels and gold and silver.

Faran could not believe what he was seeing. Stacked careless on the floor was wealth enough to buy Dromdruin a thousand times over. No, there was wealth enough here to buy Faladir, and all within it, a thousand times over. It would make the king look a pauper, and they had only just entered this place. The wide corridor continued far out of sight beyond the light of Kareste's staff.

He looked at Ferla. He saw wonder on her face also. But it was Aranloth who spoke, and his voice was grave.

"Behold! You see here the plunder of nations. This is but one of the treasuries of the Letharn. These are the spoils of but one campaign in antiquity. You may see the gleam of gold and the glow of jewels in the shadow. I see the blood of warriors spilled. Both our own, and our enemies. Or those who our greed shaped into enemies. This is not a storehouse of wealth, but a well of sin, and the dark waters of it run deep."

Faran was stupefied. This was just *one* of the treasuries of the Letharn? But the words of the lòhren made him think. All this was won by war. But perhaps that was the nature of empires. They had to expand and grow. If not, they died.

But they had died anyway. And what good was all this wealth to them now?

Kareste led them on, and the treasury continued. But after a little while, Faran stopped looking. The treasure here was more disturbing than looking at the dead.

After a while, Faran noticed a change, and he looked again. Now there were artifacts rather than treasure. There were statues and carvings. There were paintings and tapestries. There were devices of kinds that he could not guess the workings of, and vases. There were rugs and … there were weapons too.

As they moved ahead each chamber to the side was filled with swords and helms and armor. There were bows too, and maces and halberds and daggers and spears.

It struck Faran as odd that nothing here seemed to rot or decay. Especially the tapestries that he had seen before, but even the wooden handles of the weapons seemed as new, except for the dust that covered them. It could not just be the dry in this place. It was more. It was magic. He thought it was related to the harakgar, for they were the great magic invoked here, and their role of protection must extend to preservation also.

Even as he thought of the harakgar, they appeared. This time they glided upright in the air, and they came before Kareste as though to block her path.

Kareste uttered the charm, but the creatures of magic did not back away. Again Kareste voiced the words of power, and still nothing happened. It was only when she strode toward them that they dispersed in a mist that floated away, and then reformed again. Once more they took form, but they backed away as Kareste moved ahead.

"They sense our purpose," Aranloth muttered.

Kareste paused and spoke back to him. "Where exactly do we go from here, old man?"

"The next chamber on the left," Aranloth replied.

This Kareste led them to, and they entered. The harakgar hovered close all the time, and their constant presence was more than disconcerting.

The chamber was full of armor. Most was hung on stands, but some was piled on the floor.

"To the back of the room," Aranloth said.

They passed through the stands of armor. The stands looked almost like ranks of soldiers, but they did not move and the helms were hollow, being supported by thin sticks of timber. Faran felt uncomfortable though. Apart from anything else, some of the armor looked much like his grandfather's, though how that could be he did not know. This armor was ancient before Faladir was founded.

They came to the back of the chamber. There, on a stand by itself, was a silver helm and a bright sword. And a coat of gleaming chainmail.

This was not just similar to what Faran had seen, but identical to what his grandfather, Lindercroft and the king had worn.

"It's the armor of a Kingshield Knight," he whispered.

"Not just the armor of a Kingshield Knight, but the very armor that once belonged to your grandfather, and others before him."

Faran looked at him. "And this will be mine?"

"It will be yours – whether or not you become a knight. It was crafted of old, and magic is in it. Especially the sword. And you will need it. For that reason, your grandfather would have wanted you to have it."

The old man leaned wearily against his staff, and his face was gray.

"But remember this. It is not armor that makes a knight, or a warrior. It is the heart that beats within, and the skill of limb and mind that wields the blade."

Faran gazed at the armor. It seemed flawless. No nick was on the chainmail that he could see. Nor any scratch on the blade or dint in the helm. Yet he knew his grandfather had fought battles.

"Put it on," Aranloth urged him.

Faran reached for it, then hesitated. "What of the poison?"

"There is none here," Aranloth answered. "Weapons and armor might be needed swiftly, and there might be no time to cleanse them as required. So, in some few places within the tombs, that protection was not used. But I repeat, touch nothing unless I give you leave."

Kareste moved over to be near the old man if he needed any help, and Faran reached for the armor.

It was awkward to put it on. First, there was a padded jerkin that absorbed some of the power of blows and made the chainmail more comfortable. Then there was a belt that drew some of the weight of the armor and transferred it to the hips so it was light to wear. Next came the helm, and last the sword which Ferla helped attach by a short strap to the belt.

Faran felt uncomfortable and a little stupid, but Ferla stepped back and she looked at him seriously. That made him feel better.

"What of Ferla?" he asked. "Where's her armor?"

"I have not forgotten," Aranloth said. "We'll find something for her in the next chamber."

They moved out then, and Kareste continued to support the old man while Faran got used to his armor. It was strange to think that his grandfather had worn it. And reassuring. But he would *not* follow in his footsteps.

The next chamber was quite similar. It was filled with armor on stands and weapons. But again, Aranloth seemed to know exactly where he was going, and he led them to the left side, near the wall.

Here were rows of armor, but both helms and chainmail coats were smaller. Faran realized these must have been for women.

"All these suits of armor look so much the same," Faran asked. "Do they all belong to Kingshield Knights?"

"Not a one of them," Aranloth said. "Or all of them, depending on how you look at it. You see, all these suits of armor once belonged to Letharn royalty or generals. But it is also from here that I have armored every Kingshield Knight who ever lived. You and Ferla are the first to be given this honor who are neither Letharn nor Kingshield Knight."

Faran considered that. It was an honor indeed. He touched the hilt of the sword at his waist and felt suddenly unworthy.

Aranloth drew to a stop before a stand of armor that was positioned by itself against the wall. It looked like all the others, only it was slightly smaller and upon the helm was a sign. No, Faran realized, it was a rune such as his ancestors once used before they adopted the script of the Halathrin. But what did it mean to the Letharn?

This time it was Faran who helped Ferla don the armor. But with her, she did not seem awkward as he had felt. Everything seemed to fit perfectly, and she wore it with a grace that he could not match.

"Draw the sword," Aranloth said. "Let me see you hold it."

Ferla did as asked. With a fluid motion the blade slipped from the scabbard and she held it high. It gleamed in the shadowy light, and she suddenly seemed like a hero out of legend. She looked like one born to the ways of a warrior, and the rune on her helm caught the lòhren-light and flared.

"Sheath the blade," Aranloth said. "And know that the armor you now wear belonged to one that you have met.

Be proud of that, for she was a great queen, and I think you will bring as much honor to yourself as she did in her time."

Ferla said nothing, but she nodded once to Aranloth and slid the blade home in the scabbard. But suddenly her eyes widened and she reached for the lòhren.

Faran turned to look, and he saw that the old man swayed where he stood. His face was pale as death, and only Kareste by his side kept him upright.

9. Force of Will

Faran was scared. There was something terribly wrong with Aranloth, and his breathing was ragged while his faced paled even further.

They eased him to the ground, and there he lay unmoving. Kareste held her fingers to his wrist and neck, checking his pulse, and she bent her ear close to his chest to listen to his breathing.

"What is it?" Ferla asked.

Kareste squatted back on one leg, and she shook her head slowly.

"I don't know. He was not well before, and then he fought that shadow on the bridge. It took more out of him than I knew. The use of lòhrengai is not without effort or consequences. It taxed him greatly, and he is close to death."

Faran could not believe he was hearing those words, but they matched the fear that surged through him. He had been there through the worst of his grandfather's last days, and he knew the signs of grave illness.

"Is there anything we can do?" he asked.

Kareste looked at him as though assessing exactly what he was made of, like a tool being judged for fitness to the task at hand. And especially if it would break.

"His heartbeat is erratic," she said. "I can lend him of my own power for a while, until he regains his own strength. But I cannot do that and protect against the harakgar at the same time."

She looked at Faran, her brown-green eyes boring into his own. "You must take over the charm for me, and keep the harakgar at bay until we escape the tombs."

Faran felt a cold chill sweep through him. "But I have no magic. I can't do it."

"There's no time to ease you into this, Faran. You *must* do it, or Aranloth will die. As you get older you will realize necessity makes you do things that you do not wish, or do not think you can. This is such a situation. We all must rely on you to do that task, because you are the best hope. There is no other choice."

She held his gaze a moment longer. "But you should know this, also. You have more magic than you think. As the old queen said, you have seen the Lady of the Land, and that is not by accident. But the power of the charm is also in the words. You need no magic to speak them."

Faran wanted to refuse, but he felt the truth of what she had said and straightened.

"I'll do my best."

"That will be enough. Now, repeat the charm to me."

Faran did so. He had been listening when she and Aranloth said it.

"Almost right," she said. Then she corrected some of his pronunciation.

He tried again, and she nodded. "One more time."

The charm was not hard to remember, and he voiced it again.

She flashed him a quick smile. "Good! That's it. Remember those words, and speak the charm whenever you see the harakgar. Remember also that though there is no magic from you involved, the force of your will counts. If you falter, the harakgar will swoop. Be strong!"

Faran kept a lookout then for the harakgar. They had remained outside the chamber, but he still sensed them close. Again and again, he repeated the charm in his mind, and he memorized the exact pronunciation that Kareste had taught him.

While he watched, Kareste and Ferla worked to use some padded jerkins from nearby armor and the two lòhren staffs to make a stretcher.

Kareste extinguished the light from her staff, but even as she did so she waved her hand and a mist rose from the floor that came only to their ankles but it gave off a pale light.

When they were ready, they shifted Aranloth to the stretcher and supported him by the staffs on their shoulders. Faran knew that Ferla was strong, but he had not been sure of Kareste. Yet the both of them lifted Aranloth easily.

"Time to go, Faran," Kareste said. Already she seemed distracted, and he guessed that not only would she maintain the light but that she also had begun to support Aranloth with magic and keep him alive.

"Where to?" he asked.

"Back to the main passage, and then the same way we were going before. Always head up now when there is a choice, but I should still be able to give you brief instructions as we go."

Faran squared his shoulders and led them on. But his first challenge came sooner than he expected.

No sooner had they reached the main passage when the harakgar swooped. The creatures screamed and hissed, hovering before him with those wicked knives drawn and hatred in their eyes.

"*Har nere ferork. Skigg gar see!*" Faran shouted.

The harakgar seemed to pay him no heed, and if anything they hovered closer, spittle dripping from their lips and hunger replacing hatred in their eyes.

"*Har nere ferork. Skigg gar see! Har nere ferork. Skigg gar see!*" Faran screamed the charm, and he knew he was saying it right, but still the harakgar edged closer, and he felt fear stab him as surely as those horrible knives soon would.

"Yelling does not really help," Kareste said calmly, and Faran admired her in that moment. "Say the words, and put the force of your will into them. You know the charm, and the harakgar *will* obey your will."

Faran did not look at the serrated knives in the harakgar's hands. Instead, he held their gazes in turn and softly spoke the charm, but this time he put all the strength of his will into the words.

The harakgar screamed, and they spat like a cornered cat. But they slowly backed away.

He stepped forward and moved down the corridor, and the harakgar continued to give way, but all three in unison raised their knives and slowly slit their own throats.

Blood spurted and slicked the floor. It ran in red slivers over their naked skin and down their bodies. Then they laughed madly and dissolved into a red mist that seeped into the floor and was gone.

Faran understood. These were creatures of magic, and they could be anything and take any form. They had no true substance. They could not harm themselves. But they could induce fear. More than that, they could invoke terror, and that was what they had tried to do just now.

He also understood they had sent a message. Death waited for him and his companions. The harakgar would attack and kill the moment they could do so, and it must yet be a long way out of the tombs.

With a deep breath, Faran slowly walked forward. He would see everyone out of here, and he would fulfil the trust Kareste had placed in him. As she had said, he *must* fulfil it. There was no one else to turn to and no other choice.

He moved over the stone where the harakgar had disappeared. Of the blood that he had seen, there was no sign, and he tried not to think of them lying in wait and preparing to attack. He knew the charm, and he would voice it when he saw them. That would keep them at bay, and nothing else mattered.

The strange mist-light that Kareste had summoned moved along with them as they traveled. It was eerie, but it served its purpose. Faran could see where he was going, and he could see the harakgar if they attacked. That was all the light he needed, and it was better anyway that many of the alcoves and side passages remained hidden.

Most of the time, he had no trouble finding his way. There was one main passage, and it led up. That was where he had been told to go. Kareste must have been watching him, but she did not speak or interfere in his few choices when he came to a fork or crossroad. She was busy with what she was doing with Aranloth, but had he made the wrong choice she would have spoken.

He did not set a fast pace. He was unburdened, but he was mindful that Ferla and Kareste carried the lòhren. That was no easy task, and it was uphill also. If one of them were injured or grew too weak to go on, then they were all in trouble. He would not risk that.

The underground tunnels seemed to have no end. But it was hard to measure time down here. How far they had walked, or how long, he could not tell. But he yearned to feel a cool breeze on his face and to see natural light. It did not matter if it was the sun or the moon or the stars. He just wanted to feel open spaces again.

And he wanted to be free of the dead. How many millions of corpses were there down here? How many tens of millions? Hundreds even. Nor, he knew now, were they fully dead.

The Letharn had trapped themselves. They had bound their spirits to this world. In their pursuit of life after death, they had invoked some magic that preserved them. They were not alive, but they were not quite dead either, and he wondered what other spirits roamed the darkness beneath the earth other than the old queen whose armor Ferla now wore. Would they all be friendly as she had proved?

He did not think so. The queen had said as much herself. Aranloth had enemies among his own people. He had done something long ago that a group of them considered a betrayal. But the queen did not. Faran did not know what it was, and he knew better than to ask. But he would back Aranloth's judgement. He was a good man. Not just because the legends said so, but because he had proved it himself in times of danger.

Faran strode with more purpose now. Aranloth had helped him when he needed it. Now, it was his turn to give back.

They climbed a stairwell cut deep into the stone of the earth, and then they emerged into a different type of tunnel. Maybe it was not a tunnel at all but a natural cave. The walls were rough, and the floor as well.

It was here that the harakgar came against him again. There was a rush of air and a screeching sound. But they carried no knives this time, nor did they appear as women.

The harakgar filled the tunnel as a wave of water. It rolled toward Faran, seething and hissing. White foam roiled at its crest, and the water churned like the green of a storm that brought hail.

Wind came before the wave, buffeting him. He tried to voice the charm, but the maelstrom of air and swirling dust within it filled his mouth and he could not speak.

He cowered down. But he did not retreat. In the vastness of the wave rolling toward him he saw the leering faces of the harakgar, and he saw the lust for his death in their eyes.

Once again he tried to voice the charm, but fear stilled his tongue. The wave rolled on, and in moments it would consume him and those he had been tasked with protecting.

10. You Have Met Your Match

Druilgar, king of Faladir and First Knight, still felt the pain of his sundering from the creature of magic that he had sent against Faran.

The pain was of little consequence. He was a knight, and he could endure far worse than that. No, what hurt more was the wound to his pride. He had thought the Elùdurlik, the Shadow Hunter, invincible. He had thought it sufficient for the task at hand to kill the young man and the ancient prophecy with him. But he had been wrong, and that was harder than all the pain in the world to endure.

He did not like doubt. The world was a better place when everything was certain and fitted to a precise order. Eventually, that would be *his* order. Faladir was falling into line, yet while the prophesy remained there would be those who had hope to oppose him. Hope gave them life, and he must snuff that out.

But the young man could wait. He had escaped, so far, but death would catch him sooner or later. He had eluded it by leaving Faladir, yet that was a two-edged sword. By leaving, he had also withdrawn the possibility of fueling hope. Not being there was nearly as good as being dead.

A spasm of pain wracked his brain, and then left. He did not pause as he walked, and he gave no sign of the problem to the twenty soldiers marching behind him. They must think him a god. They must think him invulnerable to the ailments of lesser men, as they must also think him all-knowing and all-powerful. If they did not already, then they would in the future.

The pain had abated little since the sundering, and it hindered his clear thinking. He would heal it, not because he could not endure it but to better fulfil his own destiny. Faladir needed him whole and functioning perfectly. And the world thereafter.

He looked forward to the touch of the stone also. The Morleth Stone. Each time he used it, he grew. It was the greatest power in Alithoras, and Aranloth would have it kept guarded and unused?

But the lòhren was an old fool. He had fought a good fight for years beyond count. But his time was over. The world was changing, and a new order was coming.

Why should the lòhrens be the guides of the land? Why should they counsel kings and wander realms dispensing knowledge and wisdom? The Morleth Knights would one day take their place. After all, the knights had been established in imitation of the lòhrens from the beginning. But the imitation could grow. There could be more than six knights, and why should they limit themselves to Faladir alone when all Alithoras would benefit from them?

It was a short distance from the palace to the Tower of the Stone. Yet twice he had nearly stumbled from the pain of the sundering. It was pride that made him delay the healing, and he could not afford pride. Everything rested on him. He must keep himself healthy. And it would be a loss to have to kill the soldiers as well. If they saw him stumble, they could not be allowed to spread word of his weakness. They were only men, and they could be replaced. But not swiftly. It took time to train a soldier well.

He approached the tower, and marveled at it. His ancestor had crafted something great here. The tower was tall, and the dark stone of its making smooth and well fitted, piece to piece, without crack. The squat barracks nearby were made of the same stone, and they were pleasing in their way. But they served only one purpose, and that was to have soldiers close at hand to help the knights guard what was inside the tower. That had been all important, and it still was. He would suffer no other hand to raise the stone save his own.

He cast his gaze upward. High above there was a window at the top of the tower, and in the room beyond was the stone. It was the great hope of humanity. He could not wait to reach it, and see it again. Even better would be to touch it, and his hand trembled at the thought.

He quickened his stride, and the tread of the soldiers marching behind him grew louder as they matched his pace.

The city around about was vague. Streets and squares and commoners looking at him in awe meant nothing. The stone was everything, and it was his. His to command. His to rule. His to hold up and strike down the enemies of mankind.

Set into the thick stone of the tower was a door, and he reached it. Once again, his ancestor had built wisely and with beauty. The door was not of wood, but dark metal infused with magic. Through all the long years not a speck of rust touched it.

On massive hinges the door rested, and covered by stone and mortar were doorposts of the same metal, sunk deep into the tower foundations to hold the weight.

But his ancestor was not perfect. Druilgar looked at the engraving on the door with distaste. It was inlaid with gold, and this contrasted well with the dark metal. But the image was of a knight sitting cross-legged. A book was in one hand and from the other light shone from the palm. It symbolized the quest for knowledge and the spreading of wisdom.

Druilgar shook his head. He was beyond emotions such as anger, but the art was stupidity itself. Better by far if the knight had been standing with his sword drawn. Wisdom availed little in the end. It was action that counted, and the willingness to enforce what was right rather than speak of it.

There was another group of soldiers standing guard at the door. These knew by now not to speak to him, but quickly and efficiently they opened the door and made way for his passing, heads bowed. No one looked him in the eye. That was not by his command, but he liked it anyway. It showed the proper respect.

With a quick gesture he commanded the soldiers following him to stand guard at the front. He would ascend the tower alone.

They closed the great door behind him, and it grew dark. The only window was far above. But the dark did not disturb him.

He had changed. He had grown under the influence of the stone. Aranloth had taught him a spell for light, which had seemed like a transformation of its own at the time. He had become greater than other men. Yet the stone had worked a true transformation, and a superior one. His eyes were altered, and he could see in the dark without the need for light at all.

He began the ascent. Eagerness grew in him, but he calmed himself and did not hurry. He took one step at a time. This he hated. The climb was long and arduous, and there was nothing to see but the winding stairwell, the circling stone of the wall and the hollow center of the tower that grew deeper and deeper.

Time passed. The only sound was at first the soft tread of his doe-skin boots. Then as he climbed, the drawing of his breath. He was too old to climb the tower, but the stone had made him young again. Even so, the effort quickened his heart and made him breathe harder. But not so hard as the other knights who at times made the same climb with him. Despite his age, he was become stronger than they.

At length, he came to the end of the staircase. Before him was a door. This one of wood, yet engraved in it and inlaid with gold just as below, was another figure. This time the knight was standing, but his head was bowed and his shoulder stooped as though he carried a heavy burden. It was supposed to symbolize the great task of the Kingshield Knights, and that the temptation of the Morleth Stone would weary them.

That was nonsense, for he had learned otherwise. The stone gave him vigor, and the image made the knights look weak. Had it appeared in public, he would have destroyed it. But here, he let it be. In time it would be seen otherwise. It would come to symbolize the burden the knights would bear in the future. The burden of spreading his rule to all lands and peoples.

Three times he knocked on the door, using the gold knocker attached two thirds the way up. The very same the first king would have used.

A voice came dully from the other side, following the ritual.

"Who seeks entrance to the enclosure of the stone?"

Druilgar gave the appropriate answer, without which the door would not be opened and a horn sounded to summon soldiers.

"A seeker of wisdom, in humility and without pride."

There was a pause, and then he heard the three great bolts that secured the door being drawn back in turn. But it did not open.

This also was part of the ritual, and for good reason.

Carefully, Druilgar pushed the door open. He did not move into the room swiftly, but instead took slow movements. It was not a time for misunderstandings.

Before him stood Savanest, one of the knights and he who today guarded the stone. His sword was drawn, and it was lifted high, ready to mete out death.

Druilgar took no offence. This also was part of the ritual of guarding the stone. The sword would not be lowered until Savanest studied him and ensured he was who he claimed to be.

There was a tense moment. Druilgar was careful to make no move and to keep his hand well away from the hilt of his sword.

With a quick movement, Savanest sheathed his blade and offered a perfect bow.

"Welcome, First Knight Druilgar," the man said by way of greeting. Within the tower, that title took precedence over being king.

"Greetings, Knight Savanest," the king replied.

Druilgar looked around the room. It had not changed since the tower was built. It was a simple room, devoid of decoration or furniture except for a desk and chair to the left where the knights could write. This was often poetry but sometimes history.

The window was small and narrow, and let in little light. Iron bars secured it. On the floor was a bearskin rug. That alone changed over the years as it was worn out by knights sitting on it and meditating.

But it was toward the far side that his gaze drifted. There, in an iron box, unadorned and rusted, was concealed the greatest treasure of Alithoras.

"Is there any news?" Savanest asked.

"Very little. Aranloth yet lives, and the young man and girl with him also."

"Then Knight Lindercroft has failed?"

Druilgar thought on that. He had been harsh with Lindercroft, but it was certainly true that Aranloth was cunning.

"He has failed. But only for the moment. I do not doubt that he will try harder in the future. At some point, he, or another of the knights, will eliminate the threat."

There was no need to mention that his own efforts had also failed.

"The signs and portents grow," Savanest told him. "Destiny draws near. Only an hour ago, while I sat meditating, the stone showed me a vision."

That focused Druilgar's attention. The last vision had been some time ago when he himself had been shown Dromdruin Village. Lightning struck it seven times, and then it sunk into the earth and was covered. The meaning had been clear. The threat of the seventh knight would originate there, and it must be destroyed.

"What did you see?"

Savanest hesitated. "I saw Osahka, and he burned in dark flames. The earth was blackened, yet his staff lay on that barren ground, and it sprouted in seven places, and from each an oak tree grew."

Druilgar considered that. He did not like it. The meaning might be that even if Aranloth were killed, the seventh knight would still rise. But he did not say as much to the other knight. Savanest would have interpreted it in similar fashion.

"We no longer use the term Osahka. Not for Aranloth."

Savanest stiffened. "It was an error, First Knight Druilgar. I did not even know that I said it. It was merely an old habit asserting itself."

Druilgar looked at him coldly. Savanest was not the only knight who found it hard to leave the past behind and embrace the future. But they all would in the end. They would have no choice, for the future was like a towering wave of the ocean. Unstoppable.

"You may wait outside until I am done," he said. "I would commune with the stone."

Savanest left quietly, and he closed the door behind him. He had been rebuked, and he would think of his own penance for his failure.

Druilgar sat cross-legged on the rug. It was time now to cast away thoughts of this mortal world and its everyday problems. Now, he must find his spiritual center and open his mind for the communion to come.

He slowed his breathing until it was so fine that not even a strand of silk suspended before his face would move. Yet still his breathing was deep. He drew on the true breath, and guided air deep into his lungs and then farther down into the har-harat, the energy center of the body below the navel.

His abdomen grew warm, and he felt the tingling of energy there immediately. But it grew stronger as his mind focused upon it. For this, the mind was key. Aranloth had taught him so, but under his guidance he had never gone beyond that. Yet under the power of the Morleth Stone, he had advanced farther.

Calmly, Druilgar shifted his focus. Now, he concentrated on the spot between his eyebrows known as olek-nas, the third eye.

The energy of his body responded. It flooded upwards and filled the olek-nas. It did not tingle so much, and there was no warmth. Yet he felt the effects of it.

His mind opened and expanded. Emotion fell away from him like the brown leaves of a tree in a sudden gust of winter wind. He was one with the world now, and there was neither fear nor hate nor love nor sadness. There was only reality, and the knowledge of the true working of the universe to a pattern of ebb and flow.

He stood in one graceful motion, and he moved with purpose but not haste toward the iron box that held the stone.

Despite the age of the box, and that rust covered and pitted its surface, the hinges had been well-oiled and the lid lifted easily at his touch.

Reverently, he gazed at the stone. It was black, yet its surface gleamed and swirled. Almost, he thought he saw something move within it, and then it was gone.

He removed the stone from the box and sat back down on the rug, holding it in both hands. It was cool to the touch, but not cold. And he sensed the magic within it flare to life.

"Osahka," Druilgar said softly. "Heal me, for I am hurt."

And the stone answered back. Its voice echoed in his mind like the combined voice of a choir, single, but made up of many.

Heal thyself, First Knight. I shall show thee the way.

Druilgar saw then a vision. A shining light lay over his mind, and the brightness of it hurt him. But a cooling darkness came, and it dulled the light.

The vision faded, and Druilgar summoned his magic. Uttering a word of power, he drew it into his mind, and there he transformed into the same darkness the vision had shown him.

His pain faded away. He was not sure, but it seemed to him that it went into the stone, and something of the stone passed into him. That might be, for no magic created anything. It took the energy of something that was there, and transformed it.

Now we must speak, brother to brother.

Druilgar listened, and the stone whispered things that he did not know. And it spoke of the sundering, and the forces unleashed when the Shadow Hunter had died, and the Ring of stones that Aranloth had used to Travel the void.

And Druilgar laughed at the end, and he replied to the stone.

"At last, Aranloth has met his match. His end will be fitting."

11. The Magic of their Making

The wave rolled toward Faran. It was not quite water. Nor was it only darkness. It was made of both, and magic infused it and the leering faces of the harakgar grew larger within it.

This was how he would die. And those with him. But even as he thought that he stiffened. He would die one day, but not like this. He was a man, and he had the strength of will of one. He was descended from a Kingshield Knight, and courage flared within him.

He flung up his hand, palm out. "*Har nere ferork. Skigg gar see!*" he cried, and the full force of his will went into the words.

The rolling wave crashed and boomed as though it had hit a cliff face, and that cliff face was Faran's will. Water foamed and seethed, repelled backward in a shifting maelstrom of confusion and disarray. The darkness within it splintered and disappeared.

So too the harakgar, and when their faces were gone, so was the illusion of the wave.

But the harakgar rose from the floor again, seeming to drip with water. Yet they stood there only, and made no move to attack.

Faran pointed at them. He was tired of their presence and their constant threat.

"Go!" he said. "There is something that follows us. Seek it and kill it. Go!"

And the harakgar went. They grew wings and sped through the air, flying well above Faran and his companions and hurtling away into the darkness beyond.

Faran looked at his companions to see that all was well, and Kareste gazed back at him, her eyes intense as she studied him.

"Let's go," he said, and he led them forward.

They marched ahead through the dreary passages. But as commanded, he ever found a way that led upward. He must have been lucky to keep picking the right pathways, for Kareste never said anything. But after some while his legs began to ache and he looked back at the two carrying the stretcher. They were doing it tougher than he was.

"Time for a rest, I think."

No one disagreed with him. Gently, they lowered Aranloth down and sat in a corridor. They were, as always, among the dead. But they had to eat and Faran dug into their supplies and shared out a quick meal.

Kareste did not speak, but she ate thoughtfully, dividing her time between studying Aranloth and studying him.

Ferla spoke little. He could see that she was tired, but he had a feeling that they must be near the surface of this dreaded place. It could not go on forever, and when they reached the outside world once more then things would be better. The fresh air would do Aranloth good, and without the fear of the harakgar hanging over them, they would all be better.

Faran was tired, and he was tempted to sleep. But there could be no sleep in these tombs. Not with the harakgar. So he stretched and rose once more.

With a sigh, Ferla also stood. Kareste had one last look at Aranloth, and checked his pulse in several places again.

"He's a little stronger," she said. Then she fixed him with those eyes again. "Just so you know, the charm only works to stop the harakgar from attacking. It gives you no power of command over them. The magic of their making ensures they cannot be controlled, only stopped from killing. Nothing else."

"I didn't know that."

"No. You did not. Yet they *obeyed* you. Or at least seemed to. Your will is strong, and that is one of the foundations of magic."

She said no more, and shifted all of her attention back to Aranloth.

Faran led them forward again, but he was thoughtful. Had Kareste been trying to tell him something?

The harakgar returned soon after that. They kept their distance though, and watched. Had they really gone in pursuit of the shadow as he had commanded? Perhaps. Or maybe they had just disappeared anyway. But if they did, could they have killed it? Anything was possible, but they had not killed it the first time so maybe they could not the second.

They kept their distance, but every once in a while they moved close. He uttered the charm though, and they were quick to retreat, if with a grudging expression on their beautiful but terrible faces.

The tunnels they followed began to rise steeply, and Faran dared hope they were close now to an exit from this place. He felt better, and even Aranloth began to improve. From time to time he even offered directions as they came to a crossroads.

"We're close now," Kareste muttered. But she still kept most of her attention on the old man, though her mood seemed to have lightened as well.

It all changed swiftly, however. Even as Faran thought he saw light ahead, which surely must mean an end to walking the tombs, the harakgar began to move again.

They did not attack, though they did draw closer. Each held one of those serrated knives in their hands, but they did not threaten Faran with them. Instead, beyond his comprehension, they turned those cruel blades on themselves.

The first one raised it with trembling hands, and slowly she drew it across her own neck. It bit deep, and a trickle of blood soon turned to a flood as it spurted from a severed artery. And she kept sawing away until her head was half severed from her body. Yet still, she slowly edged toward him, her head lolling.

The second took her knife, and one by one plucked out her eyes. She screamed as she did so, and all the pain the world had ever felt was voiced in the tombs deep beneath the earth.

The third was the worst. She traced the blade slowly across the pale skin of her belly, and then even more slowly slit herself open. The blade sawed into her abdomen, and blood began to run down her body and legs. Yet she did not stop. With the curved knife, she dug deep and then slowly pulled her own entrails out until they began to spill onto the ground. And over them she walked, edging closer.

Faran would have vomited had he not been in shock. What were they *doing?* Why would they hurt themselves?

"Faran! The charm!" Ferla screamed.

And then Faran understood. The harakgar were not hurting themselves. They could be anything and take any appearance. This was illusion, and its purpose was to shock him so deeply that he forgot to utter the charm.

"*Har nere ferork. Skigg gar see!*" he cried.

The harakgar hissed in fury. Their wounds closed over and healed. They flew up into the air, and screaming they drove into the stone roof and disappeared through it.

"Quickly!" Kareste urged. "Make for the entrance before they return."

Faran strode ahead. The light at the end of the tunnel grew rapidly, and behind him he heard Kareste and Ferla begin to run even though they carried the stretcher.

He ran too, but it was hard going. They trod now a set of ancient stone stairs, worn by time and slippery and steep.

Their breathing became ragged with effort, and then suddenly they were out. They passed through some kind of chamber, and then out through a triangular door. Early morning sunlight bathed his face, and he breathed deep of the fresh air. He felt *alive* again.

They did not go far out into the open. Kareste and Ferla lowered the stretcher, and then lay down beneath the open sky to get their breath. Faran remained standing, and he looked back at the exit through which they had passed. He saw now that they had emerged from a building, maybe a temple of some sort.

The building was of strange design, being triangular, and the windows within it were triangular also. He would not go back inside, he hoped *never* to go back inside, but curiosity drove him to look in through the exit they had rushed out of. During those last few moments he had seen some strange things.

He walked back. The building itself was made of massive granite blocks. How people had even moved such heavy objects, he could not guess. Peering inside, he saw the walls were covered with carvings.

There was a procession of men, women and children. With them were warriors and lòhrens, or maybe priests of some sort. At the head was a wagon drawn by white oxen.

It seemed that this represented some sort of funeral ceremony. That probably meant that his guess was right – the building was a temple of some kind.

In the center of the floor, near the farther entrance back into the tombs, was another one of those steles that the ancients seemed to favor. This one was as tall as a man, but thicker than it was tall. He could not make out what was carved into its sides, but he thought something was there. He was curious, but not so curious that he would venture inside again.

He turned his back on the entrance to ensure he was not tempted. It was then he realized that he could hear the roar of the great falls again, and he walked around the temple to look what was beyond it.

The temple was situated close to the escarpment, and far below was a green angle of land. He could not see the lake below the falls, but he saw the two rivers that sprang from it. They glittered silver, and he looked beyond them to the great hill where the city of the ancient Letharn had been built. It was far away, yet it still seemed vast. Once, when the city was alive, this must have been an incredible view.

He moved back then to the others. They had rested a little, and Aranloth had moved off the stretcher and was sitting cross legged on the ground.

"You're looking a lot better," Faran said.

"I feel a lot better. But if not for Kareste…"

"Leave over, old man. You're tougher than old leather. I just gave you a bit of help, that's all."

Aranloth grinned at her. "You saved my life, and if that makes you uncomfortable, you'll just have to live with it."

Kareste looked away, but Aranloth merely looked amused.

"The rest of you did well, too. Especially you, Faran. Speaking the charm is harder than it looks, yes?"

"Yes it was. The harakgar are strange and … terrible."

Aranloth nodded slowly. "That they are. And they, and the tombs, tend to suck the life out of you. The air down there is not good to breathe, and that is part of the reason I feel better now."

"But what of the shadow that you fought? Do you think it's still down there, somewhere?"

A flicker of pain passed over the old man's face. "It surely must be dead now, either by fall into the abyss or by the harakgar. Even if not, how could it find us again? The path we took is lost to it, and how could it pick up our trail again in there? It could wander around for months before it stumbled across it."

That made sense to Faran, but doubt still nagged at him. He saw that same doubt on Aranloth's own face, too.

12. Battle Will be Rejoined

Lindercroft felt fury rise in him like a storm. Aranloth had escaped, and made him look like a fool. He uttered words of power, and loosed his temper upon the world.

A great wind roared to life, and it sped up the long slope of the hill tearing the fog to shreds. He should have sensed the old man's hand in the concealment it gave, and divined his purpose.

The wind reached the summit, and men hunkered down before it. Turning and twisting, it whined through the standing stones and made them sound like shrieking spirits, standing tall and defying all that came against them. Then the wind sped up into the heavens and faded away.

When it grew still again, men straightened and cast furtive glances at him. He did not care. Nor had the fury that was inside him found proper release.

He ignored everything, and studied only the standing stones, trying to regain his calm. It had been a long time since he had given in to human emotions such as anger, and it shamed him that he had now. But that shame only seemed to fuel his anger all the more.

The stones were the key. He disregarded all the men around him, and that they had seen his failure. He must focus his thoughts and think clearly.

Of Rings such as these, he had heard tell. Stories and legends for the most part. But he had read of them too. He did not think Aranloth had ever mentioned them though. And that was typical. *You are not lòhrens*, he used to say to the knights. Whenever he had given knowledge, he had held it back also. But who was he to decide what a knight needed to know?

Lindercroft began to calm himself and to think clearly. The scent of magic was still strong in the air, and it had been very powerful. He thought back to what he had seen, and he knew this must have been Traveling. How it worked was beyond him. He could understand the principles, but the specific knowledge of how to make it work was in the details.

Those details belonged to the lòhrens, and the lòhrens alone. He would not ever learn them, nor the other knights. Therefore, the Ring was an asset only to the enemies of the knights.

The ring had to be destroyed. If he could not use it, he would ensure that no other could.

He looked around, and saw the closest captain. He beckoned him over, and he saw that the man came reluctantly. That was his own fault for displaying anger. A leader of men had to be better than that.

Lindercroft returned the man's salute. "Be at ease, Captain. I have a task for you."

"What task, my lord?"

"Gather your men. Have them cast down every stone in this Ring."

The captain gazed over at the standing stones. "It'll take time. Those stones are large, and their bases are probably buried deep in the earth."

"Then take time! We have enough of it."

The captain saluted silently, and then left to give orders. Lindercroft turned away from both him and the stones. He *must* regain control of himself. This was not fitting, and he would have need of these men in the future. He could not apologize, but he must ensure that he treated them well from this point onward. The fault had not been theirs, but his. And a leader of men without their loyalty was vulnerable.

The captain broke the men into groups, but only so many men could work at once on the stones. And there were no shovels available. Timber would have to be sought and cut into digging sticks, and the men were useless until that was done. Even then, the captain was correct. The base of the stones would be buried deep. But time was not the issue now. He had to think before he could decide on his next course of action.

His anger ebbed away as a new thought came to him. Something had happened just at the end. A summoning of some sort had leapt into the circle of stones and then Traveled with Aranloth and the others. Surely that was the creature sent by the king to kill the boy and the girl?

Were his enemies dead? It was possible. Likely even that some of them were. But there were two lòhrens present, and they were formidable. He must assume until he knew otherwise that the threat to Faladir remained.

But what should he do now? He dared not return to the city. Not after his failure. He must assume the threat persisted and try to find the boy, or at least signs of where they had Traveled to and been killed by the summoning. He must still kill them all, or find proof of their death. Only then would he return to Faladir.

His mind was made up. He would establish a base camp on this hill, and he gave orders to that effect. Then, as the elù-draks came and reported to him, he would give them new instructions. They must go far abroad and scour the land looking for their enemy. In particular, they must concentrate their efforts wherever there was a circle of standing stones.

Normal scouts could not cover anywhere near as much ground as the elù-draks, but he had men at his disposal and he would use them. They might find something the elù-draks did not, and they could talk to people, which his other searchers could not. That way, he may trace rumor of travelers. Even in the wild lands there were small villages and hunters.

But first, he must report to Druilgar. It was not something he wished to do. He had failed. Yet he must. But that did not mean he had to do so straight away.

The rest of the day passed in a flurry of activity. The men were busy, but it would still take until the end of tomorrow at least before the stones were cast down. While some were working on that, others established the camp, and at its center was Lindercroft's tent. He moved into it as soon as it was erected, but he waited until night fell, he had eaten, and the last reports and scouts came in before he readied himself to speak to the king.

The ritual was familiar to him now, and sitting cross legged in the center of the tent he was as prepared as he could be when the vision of the king blossomed before his eyes.

Druilgar seemed older, or ill. There was a troubled look in his bloodshot eyes, and a hint of pain in his expression. It was no wonder, for the rumor among the knights was that a summoning took great effort, and that the king was linked to it. But what if it were killed? Would not the broken magic whip back on the summoner like a willow branch bent away and then released? If so, it might mean that Aranloth had defeated the king's own efforts.

"Hail, my king!" Lindercroft said.

The king gazed at him with brooding eyes. "You have failed, yet again," he said.

"It is so," Lindercroft answered. "I have failed, and I bring shame to the knights."

Even as he said that, he wished he had answered differently. If the king had also failed, had he not also brought shame upon the knights?

"We will discuss your punishment shortly. For now, what steps are you taking?"

"I am casting down a ring of ancient standing stones. I believe Aranloth used them to Travel. That was how he and his companions escaped. Where he went, I cannot determine. But I have already sent elù-draks abroad to seek signs of him in the land. And I have sent men out also. Both to search and to seek news from any that may have seen or heard rumor of the lòhren or those with him."

Druilgar listened attentively, his bloodshot eyes focused.

"You are correct. He Traveled, and he went to a far larger ring of standing stones. Where that is, I cannot say. But it was surrounded by ruins."

Lindercroft was glad of that information. There were standing stones in many places all over Alithoras. And ruins too. Yet that knowledge would still speed his search.

Druilgar had not finished speaking though. "I will assist you. There are men in my employ who are well traveled and knowledgeable of other realms. I will send them to you, and thereafter they can scatter across Alithoras seeking information."

"That will be most welcome, my lord." Lindercroft knew who these men would be. Spies. He had little liking for those who practiced the arts of subterfuge, yet he could not deny their usefulness.

"This also I shall do. Savanest has been too long in the tower, and he is due relief from the duties of guarding the stone. He will also scour the land with soldiers from the army. He will act independently of you though."

Lindercroft bowed his head in acknowledgment and hid his chagrin. Another knight working on this task meant that his own chances of completing it were halved.

Always, the king set the knights in competition with each other. That competition was fierce, for they each wished to prove themselves. Success in any task meant greater time with the stone. It was a reward to guard it, but also an opportunity to grow in power by virtue of proximity. Just being in the tower seemed to bring greater health and strength in magic. It had even brought youth back to the king, but he was jealous of it too. He kept the knights vying for the privilege and in constant rotation. They whispered amongst themselves that he wished none of them to spend too long there lest they grow in power enough to match his own.

"What of the summoning you sent to destroy them, my lord? I saw it leap into the Ring just as they began to Travel. What happened to it?"

It was a foolish thing to ask. He knew now it must be dead, but it was a way to fight back against the king. That thought too was foolish. Everything he had, or was, stemmed from the king. At least, while the king possessed the stone.

"The elùdurlik perished," Druilgar answered. "It was destroyed by lòhren-fire and arrow. This much I learned from its passing though. The boy and the girl have great courage. And…"

Druilgar's voice trailed away as though he were in thought or had realized something for the first time and only now had begun to contemplate it.

"What is it, my lord?"

The king's gaze flicked back to him, those bloodshot eyes intense.

"There were great forces unleashed when my summoning leapt into the circle of stones. Such Rings tap into the vast power of the earth. Then there was Aranloth's lòhrengai to activate it. And finally the beast itself, which was born by the power of the stone. Those three forces swirled together into the void, and then came out somewhere else in Alithoras. But they had to have interacted in some way. Something unexpected must have come from that."

"How do you know, my lord?"

"I do not. But instinct tells me it is so, and my instincts are sharper and reach farther than they ever have before." The king ran a hand through his long white hair. "This much is certain though. The battle will be rejoined. Either we will find our enemies, or our enemies us. For Aranloth will not abandon Faladir indefinitely." He paused, quickly removing his hand from his hair as though he had made a decisive decision. "Now, it is time to mete out your punishment."

13. A Peaceful Land

Aranloth regained strength, albeit slowly. The travelers stayed by the temple all day, and the night after.

But dawn of the next day saw them moving off once more. Aranloth was strong enough to walk, and he led them. He set a slow pace though, one arm in a sling and the other using his staff as a walking stick. Their rest breaks were frequent, too. This was far different from the way he had led them out of Dromdruin, but Faran was just glad to see that he was improving.

Perhaps given time, the old man would be as he was. But there was still a shadow of pain on his features, and the way that he needed his staff to aid balance was worrisome.

They headed south, and the country was an undulating one of open grasslands. But small stands of trees were numerous, some even large enough to be called a wood. There were few pines, and the trees were often oaks, but there were many broadleaf varieties whose names Faran did not know. This land had the look about it of fields that had once been cultivated, but that the forest was claiming back.

"Where are we going?" Faran asked as they commenced to walk once more after a break. It was not that he really cared. Everywhere was new to him, and anywhere was better than where his enemies had been seeking him out.

"I know a place," Aranloth told him. "A good place. It's not far from here, and there's a cabin there that will give us shelter. There'll be game too, for we'll soon need supplies. And there's good water as well."

"The water sounds good," Kareste said. "I could do with a bath."

"Me as well," Ferla said.

Faran glanced at her. It still seemed strange to see her in chainmail. But he supposed he must look strange to her too.

They traveled at a leisurely pace for two days. Aranloth, despite his infirmity, had lost none of his wits. There was no threat that they knew of, yet still he chose paths that led them over hard ground that would leave less of a trail, and he used creeks when they came across one to hide their trail altogether.

It was still early in the morning when they approached a ridge higher than the others they had found in this undulating countryside. Trees grew on its crest, and when they reached that and looked down into the valley beyond, it seemed that the grass was greener than it had been and that there were many little woods, more numerous than the surrounding areas.

But it was the lake at the center of the valley that drew their eyes. It was not especially large, but it glittered silver and lay still in the quiet of the dale.

Faran was a hunter rather than a fisherman, but he had still caught many a fish back home in Dromdruin, and he knew that the lake would provide a quick and easy supply of food. Fishing was easier than hunting, if just as unreliable.

"This will be our home for some while," Aranloth said. "I have been here before, and I liked it. I think you will too."

Faran thought the lòhren was right. This was a peaceful land, and his enemies had lost his trail and would struggle to find him here. It was not Dromdruin, but it looked a good place to put down roots and forget the dangers that lay behind him, and that might one day catch up with him. But looking down into the valley, he hoped that day was long away.

They descended slowly. There was no trail, and it seemed that people never came here. Yet Aranloth had said there was a cottage, so it must have been populated at some point.

They passed through some woods, and these were cool with the night air still trapped within them. Faran noticed stands of hazelnuts, as well as various berries, and that would be a supply of food later on as well. Not to mention that there would be mushrooms in places like this. Food would not be an issue in this valley, and there was sure to be game as well, just as Aranloth said.

After some time they reached flat ground at the bottom. The grass was lush here, for the soil was fertile due to flooding. Spring melts would have deposited topsoil from the higher slopes for millennia.

The lake was not quite still when they came to it. The surface rippled slightly as a cool breeze blew over it, refreshing and sweet to breathe. Faran could not tell how deep it was, but he had a feeling that at its center it was very deep indeed.

Toward the edges there were shallow stretches where he could see the bottom, and at times schools of small fish darted, turned and flashed beneath the clear water.

They followed the edge of the lake, which was often sandy but at times the green grass grew right up to the water as well.

Aranloth knew exactly where he was going, and he led them after a little while to a slight rise above the lake. It was still close, but it would offer a view over the whole body of water and of the valley all around. And at the crest of that rise was the cabin he had mentioned.

Trees surrounded it, and would likely hide it from the ridges of the valley above. Certainly he had not seen it from up there. That would have been a factor that influenced Aranloth's choice in coming here. Not to mention the abundance of wild food.

The cabin was rustic, even by the standards of Dromdruin. The walls were of felled logs, though they were well chosen and neatly cut so that they fitted snugly. What gaps there were had been filled by a mixture of clay and straw. This would keep the weather out and the warmth in.

Faran glanced up. The roof was of slate, and it was pitched high to shed snow. Slate was a common enough material for roof tops, but this was old and mossy, and it blended in well with the green round about. Perhaps that was an accident or perhaps not. He began to wonder how Aranloth knew of this cabin and what it had been used for in the past.

The lòhren went to the front door, which was a sturdy construction of heavy oak boards. Far heavier, in fact, than necessary. Faran realized this place had been built with not just a mind toward concealment but also to defense.

Three times Aranloth struck the tip of his staff against the door.

"Ho the cabin!" he called.

He waited a few moments, then called again. "Ho the cabin!"

No one stirred. "Best to be careful about these things," the old man said. "I didn't expect anyone to be here, but if some traveler was using it, it's best to announce yourself. It saves getting a knife in the belly by just storming in unannounced. Folks can be touchy living out in wild lands such as this."

He turned the knob and pushed the door open. It swung smoothly on well-greased hinges, and again Faran was suspicious. From the outside, it looked like no one had lived here in decades. Yet someone must have been here in the last year or so to grease those hinges.

The floor inside was hardpacked clay sealed with some sort of oil. It was smooth and even, and in winter straw could be layered over it to keep out the cold, although that would probably not be necessary.

There was a solid wooden table with several chairs on one side. Near it was a stone hearth for cooking and warmth with a well-crafted chimney. On the other side was a series of racks and hooks in the ceiling designed for storing fruits, vegetables, sausages and cured meats.

"It'll need a good clean," Kareste said.

Faran knew she was right. But this had the feeling of home about it. He liked it instantly, and he saw Ferla looking around curiously too. He could tell that she liked it.

"There's more," Aranloth said. He went to the back wall and opened a door there. Beyond was a narrow corridor and three small rooms. None had beds, but there were piles of straw and neatly folded blankets.

Outside and around the back was a small shed, and they found many tools here, mostly for gardening, but they also found some straw brooms and rags for cleaning.

They worked for the rest of the morning, cleaning and tidying things up. Against one side of the cabin was a pile of split timber for the hearth, and Faran brought some inside in preparation for lunch and dinner. He had noticed an axe in the shed, and likely it would be his job all through the summer to find and split logs to build that wood pile high to prepare for winter. Likely, it would not get quite so cold here as in Dromdruin, but it would certainly snow.

He and Ferla would have to hunt well too. If they could obtain salt somehow, they could cure meat to last them all through the winter.

Aranloth started a fire in the hearth, after checking the chimney was not blocked, and he found various pots and pans hanging on hooks nearby and began to clean them by boiling water inside.

Soon after, they sat around the sturdy table and ate a simple meal of some of the last of their supplies.

"This will be a good place to stay," Aranloth said. He looked at Faran and Ferla in turn. "Here, in peace and quiet, we can all recuperate. And I'll teach you the skills of the Kingshield Knights."

After they had lunched and rested, Aranloth took Faran and Ferla outside and walked the short distance to the lake. They found a nice patch of grass, level and green, and an oak tree close by that threw shade to protect from the afternoon sun. There were several log seats here as well. Someone in the past had obviously favored this spot.

"I'll train you hard," Aranloth said, sitting down on one of the logs. He still looked very weak. "If you have the ability, you'll increase your skills fast. But you must put in tremendous effort. Are you willing?"

"I'm willing," Ferla said immediately.

Faran sensed an eagerness about her. "As am I," he added.

"Then let's begin." The old man gestured to Faran. "Sit and watch. I'll give Ferla a sparring partner."

Even as Faran sat down he saw an image form. It was an armed man, and he held a sword in his hand. It was not as large as the swords of the Kingshield Knights, nor did he wear armor or even a helm. He was simply dressed in doe-skin boots and gray trousers and tunic. Over that, he wore a forest green cloak with the hood up.

Faran's eyes widened in surprise. Woven in red thread on the cloak, near the heart, was a trotting fox looking back over its shoulder.

"He's a Raithlin," Ferla said. Faran knew it too, and he was surprised. They were legendary scouts, and no doubt skilled at fighting too. Too skilled for either him or Ferla.

"Not just a Raithlin," Aranloth said, "but Lanrik himself."

Ferla leveled a cool gaze at the old man. She had heard of Lanrik. He was a legend.

But it became apparent that this was no harsh fight as it had been the last time they did this. Lanrik moved in, lithe and graceful. Metal clanged against metal and he withdrew, even though he could have pressed home the attack and perhaps won the fight.

Faran understood. This was less a fight and more a sparring session. It was to give Ferla a sense for how a great warrior moved. To learn by watching and feeling.

Ferla darted in, thrusting swiftly with her blade. The Raithlin moved back gracefully, but only just enough to avoid her thrust. This positioned him well to counterstrike, which he did with a two-handed blow at her head which nearly missed, but not quite. The tip of his sword screeched against her helm and she stumbled back, far less gracefully than her opponent had retreated.

This was a great opportunity to learn how to fight, and just as much for Faran as Ferla. By watching, he could study and learn. Already he realized the importance of a good retreat. The idea was to move back just enough and no more. Otherwise you were too far away to attack in your turn. And he sensed the old man watching him nearly as much as the fight. He was making sure the lessons were observed.

"Hold your sword with a looser grip," Aranloth called. "It'll help you relax your whole body. Fighting is an art of skill, not brute strength. Only tighten your hand at the moment of contact. That'll stop the weapon being jarred from your grip."

The two combatants circled each other. Faran watched, amazed by how lifelike the illusion of Lanrik was, and also at the man's poise.

Ferla attacked again, launching a series of lightning fast strikes, but Lanrik glided away from them smoothly and then retaliated with his own offensive.

The Raithlin's movements were sure and smooth. Twice he struck Ferla's helm, and a third slash ran across her legs but the blow was held back. Ferla stumbled and fell, while the Raithlin sheathed his sword and stood motionless.

"That's enough for you," Aranloth said. "You did well against a great fighter. Some of your opponents so far have been more skilled than any Kingshield Knight. I've done that so that you can see how great the gap is between where you are and where you need to be. But don't be disheartened. Even warriors such as Brand and Lanrik once had less skill than you do now. With training, you can become formidable in your own right, and quickly."

Faran had his turn next. He tried to move with his opponent's grace, and he tried to put into place the advice that Aranloth gave him and the things he had learned by watching Ferla's efforts. But it was one thing to understand something and another to put it into practice with a sword slashing toward his head.

He did not do as well as Ferla, and his admiration of her increased. She did have genuine skill, and more than his own.

After the third time the Raithlin's sword rang against Faran's helm, Aranloth made a gesture and the illusion of Lanrik swirled his green cloak and faded away.

"Both of you," Aranloth said, "did well against an opponent that far surpassed you. You could not hope to win, but fighting a better opponent exposes your weaknesses and shows you where you must improve."

Aranloth stood up, and he led them right to the edge of the lake.

"You were both too eager to attack. Remember always that it is easier to defend than to attack, but that takes patience. This next skill of the knights well help you with that."

They followed his lead and sat cross legged on the green grass, gazing out over the tranquil lake.

"Breathe deep of the air," Aranloth told them. "But very slowly."

This they did, and Faran found it harder than it seemed. To do something slowly was often harder than to do it at speed.

"Concentrate your mind on the spot just two finger widths below your navel. The ancients called this the har-harat. Think of nothing else but slow, deep breathing, and drawing the air down to that one point. Everything else will fall away from your mind. Think only of this…"

They did as he asked, but Faran had trouble. He heard birds call in some distant trees. A fish leaped in the water of the lake and an insect chirped away in a bush nearby. But at times too these things faded and all that he thought of was the breathing.

"You cannot breathe air down to below your navel," Aranloth told them. "But by concentrating on it, it feels as though you can. The rest of the world drops away, and you know nothing but the sense of the flow of air, in and out, and always your mind is on the har-harat. When you can do this all distractions fade away. When you can do this, then it need not be the har-harat that you concentrate on. It might be a tongue of flame. Or a flower. You might be sitting as we are now. Or you might be standing or walking. Or you might have a sword in your hand and be in battle. When you can do this, then your mind and body are unified and able to devote all to one purpose without other thoughts or distractions. If you are in a fight, then you will not be too eager or to hesitant. You will act without hope or fear. Your only focus will be on victory, and this is an advantage over your opponent who by turns will hope to kill you and fear being killed themselves."

Faran thought on that. He understood it, but he knew also that just this one simple thing alone would take a lifetime of practice to perfect. Lindercroft and his other enemies had walked down this path for years ahead of him. The gap in skill between himself and them was vast.

14. Hunting

Faran felt the cool dawn air on his face, but he also felt the warmth of Ferla's body close to his own, and he liked it.

They lay in concealment beneath a spreading oak tree, a patch of ferns about them hiding their presence even more. But it was the breeze, blowing from the east, that would hide them best of all. For there were deer in that direction, and they would struggle to scent the presence of two people if they came this way to graze in the grassland beyond the oak.

It was a big if. But there were signs they came here often enough, and they had not yesterday nor the day before. Today, they might. Or not. Hunting was a gamble.

He and Ferla had been out, hunting and gathering for a week with little success, and their supplies of food were running very low. But they had caught fish in the lake, which had tied them over well enough.

Ferla shifted next to him, and he saw that she was notching an arrow to the string of her bow. What had she seen?

He gazed carefully through the half-light of a rising dawn, but saw nothing. Yet she knew what she was about, so if she notched an arrow so would he.

It was silent and peaceful all about them. From time to time a bird called, but it was still too dark for the dawn chorus. He moved slowly and silently, as Ferla had done, and then he waited.

They did not speak. They had not for several hours, but the easy quiet between them was comfortable. They were both hunters. Sometimes, they preferred silence. In a way, they were never closer than when they did not talk. Perhaps talking just got in the way.

He was glad not to be wearing his armor. Aranloth had instructed both he and Ferla to wear it at all times in order to get used to it. But hunting was an exception. Hunting required stealth, and armor made too much noise.

At length, he saw what Ferla had seen before him. There was movement on the fringe of the grassland. A doe moved cautiously into the open. She grazed for a moment, then her head came up again, ears twitching. A good while she stood like that, then she stepped forward and grazed again.

Faran could see better now. Dawn had broken, and with it came several more deer, all working their way across the grass carefully. One was a young buck, shorter in the neck and snout than the doe had been. It also had a flatter head between the ears – another sign that it was a buck. This was the one that Faran watched most closely.

There were some that said does made better eating. That was not the case in Faran's experience, nor had many hunters that he had talked with ever claimed there was much difference either way.

The buck came closer, grazing at whiles and watching the land about intently. Its ears flicked, listening for signs of danger that eyes could not discern. A moment it stood still, then it stamped a foreleg to dislodge flies. At just that moment Ferla rose up slowly, just enough to draw her bow, and loosed her arrow.

Faran did not interfere. She had seen the deer first, and it was her shot. She was nearly as accurate as he was, and if he had moved as well there was double the chance the buck would have bolted.

The world stood still a moment. The arrow was lost from sight, for it was not fully light yet, then the buck leaped in the air and sprang away.

But it was dead only a few paces later. It had been a good and clean shot, the arrow taking it through the heart.

The remaining deer scattered and were gone. "About time," Ferla said. "We haven't had much luck lately."

That was true, but their luck had just changed. There was good meat here, and plenty of it. But also the hide would be used and even sinews. The sinews were necessary for hunting – they secured arrow heads and fletching to shafts. They were also used on bows as backing to increase strength and resilience, though he used more of it for that than Ferla.

They loped across the dew-wet grass toward the kill. It had been a forty-yard shot, the farthest that either he or Ferla would attempt. Beyond that, the chances of wounding but not instantly killing the deer escalated, and most ethical hunters would not risk such a shot. Unless driven by hunger.

Together, they lifted the animal and moved it to the closest tree. There Ferla drew out her arrow while Faran worked to tie cord around the hind legs. When he was done, they hoisted it up and secured the cord over a large branch. Then Ferla, deftly using her knife, cut the animal's throat to bleed it. Doing so would help ensure the meat lasted longer.

Ferla inspected her arrow while they waited. There was some damage to it, but it would be repaired and used again.

The sun rose higher. From where they were, high up on the north side of the valley, they had a good view. But it was obscured just now by the stand of trees.

Their hunting was done, so Ferla cleaned her arrow and they unstrung their bows. It would be later in the morning by the time they got back to the cottage with the meat, but no doubt, after lunch, Aranloth would begin their training again. It would be a long day.

When the carcass was bled, they set about butchering it. This was necessary to lower the temperature of the meat quickly and help preserve it. It would also ease their burden in carrying it back to the cottage.

For a good while they worked, and once more they spoke little. It was best to get this job over quickly, for the sooner they were done the sooner they could get home, hang the meat in the shed out back where there were hooks, and then clean up.

Soon they were done. Further breaking up of the carcass could be carried out when they got home. They had found hessian bags in the shed, and these they had washed in the lake and dried. Now they used them to hold the large slabs of meat, and set out for the long walk home with their heavy load. They had tied the bags together by their cords, and used those same cords to tie the bags to a long pole, which they hoisted onto their shoulders.

Ferla led the way, and Faran followed. They would feast tonight, and all of them would also be busy making sausages to cure in the smoke by the hearth and preserve larger cuts of meat. In the shed were barrels where brining could be done, and a supply of salt that they had found. Though it was doubtful there was enough there to carry them through the winter.

They moved down the valley slope, and despite that they had worked hard, Ferla set a fast pace. She was keen to get home and wash up, and Faran did not blame her. His own hands and arms were smeared with dry blood.

But even as Faran wanted to get home, he took pleasure in being alone with Ferla now. It was almost like being back at Dromdruin before all their troubles began. Almost. But they were closer now than they had been then. What had happened had bonded them, and what they had endured and risked for each other since had bonded them even more.

His mind leaped back to what the queen had said in the tombs. *The quiet one whose name will echo through the land.* He had no idea what that meant. But he felt it was true. There was something about her, some quiet dignity and resilience that set her apart from others. She was different, and he admired her as well as liked her. She had been marked for something great, and he knew it.

The queen had also said she had a task. What it could be, Faran did not know. But he knew he would be there to help her just as she would always be there to help him.

They moved down lower into the valley, passing through fields and little forests. The sun was well up now, but the valley still seemed cool. It would grow warmer swiftly though, and Faran was looking forward to a swim in the lake. That too, Aranloth had told them, was part of their training. It developed muscles that otherwise they would not work, and it was good for relaxing strained muscles as well after their intensive training.

Ferla interrupted his thoughts. "There's trouble ahead," she whispered.

They were close to the cabin now, and as they lowered their burden of meat, Faran saw what had sparked her comment, and he felt a stab of fear run through his body.

In front of the cabin a wagon was drawn up, and that meant someone had found them.

"No one could have tracked us here," Ferla said.

"It could be a coincidence," Faran replied. But his heart was not in that answer. He no longer believed much in coincidences.

They moved the meat into the shade beneath some trees, and looked at each other. They both knew what had to be done. Aranloth and Kareste were inside, and if their enemies had found them they would need help.

15. Tidings of the Land

Faran and Ferla restrung their bows and stalked close to the cabin. This was not easy, for there was little to no cover to offer concealment that close to the building. Once more, Faran got the sense that this cabin was more than it appeared. Every aspect of it seemed planned out in detail like a military expedition.

They drew close. There was no sign of anyone at the narrow windows, so likely they had not been observed yet. They moved quickly to stand beside the cabin walls which would make it hard for them to be seen. Then they edged closer to a window to listen in case anyone was speaking.

Someone was. An old man laughed, but it was not Aranloth. He said a few muffled words as well, but they could not catch them. He must have been at the far end of the cabin near the table.

Faran and Ferla exchanged a glance. There was no indication of trouble here, of their enemies having found them. But if not, who was the old man in there? And was he alone?

There was only one thing to do. "I'm going inside," whispered Ferla. Faran nodded. He would be only one step behind her.

They moved closer to the door. It was open, but that was normal. Again, there was a muttering of voices, but nothing distinct. Faran thought he heard Kareste's voice, but he could not be sure.

Ferla strode through the door, and Faran followed. Aranloth and Kareste sat at the table, and they were smiling. With them also sat an old man. He wore brown trousers and a brown tunic. Neither looked particularly clean, and his white hair and long white beard were unkempt. He looked up from what he was eating, and his gaze took in the strung bows instantly, but he ignored that and looked at their faces instead.

"The hunters return," Kareste said. "Still no luck?"

"They had luck," the stranger said. "But they left their catch outside while they came in to check who I was, and what I was doing."

Faran felt embarrassed. Their precautions seemed unnecessary now, even rude. But the stranger had said the words as though he approved of their actions. And his eyes had been sharper than Kareste's. He had noticed the residue of dried blood on their hands.

"This is an old friend of mine," Aranloth told them. "Jareck, this is Faran and Ferla."

"Pleased to meet you," Jareck said.

They gave their own greetings. "We best put our catch in the cool of the shed," Faran said.

He and Ferla went outside and unstrung their bows. "I feel like an idiot," Faran told her.

Ferla grinned at him. "Better safe than sorry. But that Jareck has sharp eyes. He saw our strung bows and knew what it meant. But he just ignored them."

They gathered up the meat again, and then took it to the shed out back. It was cool in there, shaded by bushes from the sun and the roof covered over with sod. They worked quickly to hang the meat. It would tenderize that way, and then later they would brine it in the barrels.

Out the back of the shed was a well, dug deep Aranloth had said. It never went dry, and they hauled a few buckets of water up into a trough and washed themselves. It was still early for lunch, but with a stranger there they would eat something, and they were ravenous. Hunting was long and hard work for the most part. It certainly had been today, and Faran felt tired.

They went back into the cabin. The stranger had finished eating, but he still sat at the table. Kareste motioned them to join him.

Aranloth still sat at the table too. "Jareck is a tinker," the lòhren said. "He can fix anything from a broken axle on a wagon to a boat's rudder. But better than that, he's a storyteller and a news-bringer."

Jareck scratched his face through his beard. "Folks like things mended, but when that's done they like a story for entertainment afterward. Even more than that, they like to hear the gossip of the land. That they like best of all."

The stranger glanced at their hands, and saw that they were now clean.

"Looks like you had a good kill. In my wagon I have supplies as well. No point traveling around without bringing people things they're willing to pay for. So I have salt for curing, which Aranloth tells me you're short of."

"We are," Ferla said. "But I'm not sure if we have any money to pay for it."

Jareck shrugged. "I don't charge lòhrens. No one in the land does. Besides, I owe Aranloth. So the salt, and whatever else you need, is free."

Faran got the feeling that this man really did know Aranloth well. At least, he knew his real name which was something that all of Dromdruin did not.

"What news is there in the land?" Aranloth asked. It seemed to Faran a normal question, but he did not doubt that Aranloth was looking for news out of Faladir in particular.

Jareck leaned back and filled and lit a pipe by holding it to an ember in the hearth.

"There's lots of news," he said. "Alithoras is full of it these days."

He puffed on his pipe contentedly. "There's a new king in Cardoroth, but that's fairly old news now. But he rules well, according to the stories, and Cardoroth prospers."

"What of Brand?" Ferla asked.

"He's returned to the lands of the Duthenor, and won a great victory it seems. But he did not linger there. He took men with him and headed north into the mountains, but no news has come to me after that." He looked at Aranloth carefully. "But you knew all that, did you not?"

"All but the last," Aranloth replied. "I'm a lòhren, and news has a way of finding me. You know that."

"News and trouble both," Jareck said with a wink.

Something was troubling Faran. "If you're a tinker and a trader, why come to this valley? There's no one here beside us, and we just got here."

Jareck stretched his legs out under the table and took a long puff of his pipe.

"I often come through here. Sometimes there are folks who need what I have. Other times this cabin is empty. See, far as I can tell the lòhrens use this place as a sort of hiding house. When someone is in trouble and needs to disappear, they bring them here. Likely enough, they have other places like this all over the land."

It all suddenly became clear to Faran. Jareck was right, and this place was built for the purpose he said. It explained why it was so well hidden away, and so defendable if found.

Jareck took another puff of his pipe and fixed Faran with his eyes.

"It seems to me that you and the lass are just the sort of folk who the lòhrens hide. But old Jareck doesn't ask questions or want to know the answers. It's safer for me that way. Besides, it's easier to get a secret out of a tree stump by the side of the road than prise information out of Aranloth."

Faran glanced at Aranloth, but said nothing. If the lòhren wanted to tell this man who they were, he was welcome to. He knew Jareck well enough to decide whether or not to trust him. He and Ferla did not.

But the trader went on as if he really did not want an answer, and maybe that really was the safest way for him.

"The land hereabouts is quiet. Mind you, that's to be expected. Few people live in these parts. I'll not get rich peddling odds and ends around here. I hear tell there's trouble brewing in Faladir. Some strange stories have come out of there lately, but whether they be true or not, I can't say."

"Best assume they are," Aranloth said. "I'd stay clear of Faladir, if I were you."

Jareck glanced at the lòhren and puffed thoughtfully on his pipe. He gave no answer, but he nodded slightly to himself as though his own thoughts had been confirmed.

Kareste brought some food over to the table, hot from a pan on the hearth.

"You'll be staying for the night?" she asked.

"If there's room for me, I'd be obliged. But I'll be away first thing tomorrow."

"There's room enough, and food enough now, too," she said.

Faran and Ferla ate their meal, and they listened to the old stranger talk. He had a simple and easy-going manner about him as he told more news of the land. But his mind was sharp, and Faran saw why he was a friend to Aranloth. He seemed not only smart, but dependable and trustworthy.

After lunch, he and Ferla went out back again and got barrels ready for brining meat. They had just enough salt for the task, but they would be glad if the trader had more. It would be a long winter here in the valley, and they would need to work hard on building up a supply of food to see them through it.

When that was done, their training with Aranloth commenced again. They went to their usual spot by the lake, and there the lòhren bade them sit down facing the still waters.

He led them through the breathing training as he always did, and it was becoming more familiar to Faran. He felt as if he could begin to slow the frantic pace of the world down, and to capture some of that tranquility even during the sparring sessions that followed.

When they were done with the breathing, Aranloth summoned the illusion of a warrior as he often did. This man was tall and thin, and he had long red hair and wiry limbs full of speed and unexpected strength. But he did not have the skill of the others Aranloth had conjured.

Faran and Ferla sparred him by turns. That sparring turned into genuine-seeming fights as the session went on. But both of them beat him. He was fast and strong, but he left openings that they could take advantage of.

As they continued, Aranloth would call out instructions. He would tell them to keep their blades higher, and when to attack and when to defend. He would cause the red-haired warrior to attack them again and again in a certain fashion so they could practice the appropriate counter move.

Many of the movements they used were the same as the warrior's, and Aranloth began giving names to them that neither Faran nor Ferla had heard before. Hawk Folds its Wings. Cherry Blossom Falls from the Tree. Tempest Blows the Dust.

Faran found the names poetic, but often he also realized the names captured some essence of the move that was worthy of deep thought. And as always, Ferla was more graceful and skilled in executing them.

When they were done, Faran was feeling good. He watched as Aranloth casually gestured and the red-haired warrior faded from view.

"He wasn't as good as the other illusions you've conjured for us."

Aranloth stood from where he sat on one of the log seats.

"I try to give you variety. It's not good training to do the same thing all the time, and you were due for an easy win. But you should know this. In life, that man died in his first battle. You will have to do better than him. Or at least be luckier."

16. Words Have Power

The next morning they ate well. It was Aranloth's turn to cook, and he grilled sliced venison over a rack on the hearth. The meat could do with more aging to tenderize it, but Faran still thought it a feast. It had been a while since he had eaten fresh meat, and he especially liked the lean and strong flavor of venison.

It was just after dawn, and Jareck said he would be on his way soon. Early morning was the best time to travel, and once he had covered several miles he would feel good for the rest of the day.

But before the old man left, he opened up the back of his covered wagon. Faran was amazed at the amount of things he had stored in there. Tools and cloth and jewelry were everywhere, but there were also preserved foods and spices and all manner of strange items. He seemed able to carry more in that one wagon than had been in every cottage in Dromdruin.

He passed Faran several large sacks of salt. It would be enough to get them through the winter. To Aranloth though, he gave many tiny bags. They were vegetable seeds, and that would prove as useful as meat over time. The soil of the valley was fertile, and there was good water from the well and the lake. And it seemed as though a large area at the back of the cabin had been cultivated to a garden before. Vegetables were slow to grow, but they were far more reliable than hunting. At least, they would be with the good access to water they had.

Then Faran realized he would likely be the one to have to dig the garden, and he was less pleased. Aranloth would probably tell him it was good training for a warrior and that it built muscle.

Ferla and Kareste brought the trader's two horses out from the lean-to stable at the side of the shed, and they helped Jareck hitch them to the wagon. Then they said their goodbyes and the old man managed to whisper some private advice into his ear.

"Be friendly to all, but trust few."

It was good advice, and it seemed that the words were spoken with true knowledge behind them. Jareck was an old man, and he had traveled widely and seen many things. Then suddenly he was up in the wide driver's seat. He held the reins and loosed the break.

"Whoa!" the old man cried. "Off Strider! Off Sprinter!" The wagon lurched into motion, the two horses straining to pull it forward until it gained momentum and rolled easily.

They watched him for a good while as he skirted the lake and then moved northward up the side of the valley. Faran hoped he took Aranloth's advice and avoided even the outskirts of Faladir.

"We have meat," Aranloth said. "Now we can have vegetables too." He held up the many small bags of seeds Jareck had given him. "But what we don't have, yet, is a garden."

To Faran's surprise, this was a task Aranloth had them all work at, including himself, though he was limited in what he could do with one arm in a sling. There were various shovels, hoes and digging forks in the shed, and he set to turning over the old garden.

The work went quickly, for the soil was a good loam and had been dug before. In a short period they had it cultivated and raised into long beds. Then Aranloth planted a wide variety of seeds, knowing just by the looks of them what vegetables they were, and he marked the site of the plantings with small twigs.

He straightened up and rubbed his hands free of dirt after the last was planted.

"Time to water," he told them. But both he and Kareste went over to sit on a bench by the side of the garden.

"Looks like it's up to us," Faran muttered to Ferla.

She winked at him. "If you haul the water up, I'll get it on the garden."

For a good while after that Faran worked hard, bringing the water up from the well and pouring it into a trough made from a hollowed-out log. Ferla used her own bucket to transfer it from the trough onto the garden.

They were allowed no rest when they were done though. Aranloth took them over by the lake to their usual spot, and he led them through the breathing ritual again.

But this time he did something different. "Words have power," he said. "All words do, but the older the language spoken, and the greater the will of the speaker, the more power they have. Some words can act as a spur for magic."

Aranloth paused then, allowing them to think on this. But he continued soon after, his voice dropping low.

"Water is an example. That is your word for it, but eons before your ancestors traveled east and met the Halathrin, there was another word. *Halakness*. I want you to say that word, and feel the weight of it in your mind. Does it not give you a feeling of water itself? Does the word not roll and shift in your mind, just like water itself?"

They both repeated the word several times. Faran thought he knew what the old man meant. The word *was* the thing. Halakness *was* water.

"Now," the lòhren continued. "Close your eyes. Keep your breathing deep and slow. Reach out with your mind and feel the essence of the lake nearby. It is made of water.

Feel how the light of the sun hits its surface. Sense how it is warm there, but deep below it is cold. Sense how it moves and shifts. Feel the weight of it lying against the earth, and the wetness of it. It is Halakness. And you are one with it."

Faran felt the world come alive as the old man spoke. He felt not just the water, but the earth and the light and the air as well.

"There are forces in the world," Aranloth said. "Forces that move and substance it. In the beginning, there was only ùhrengai – the primordial power. But from this, two aspects developed. Lòhrengai and elùgai."

This Faran knew. Lòhrens used the force of lòhrengai while elùgroths that of elùgai. One was considered light and the other dark.

Aranloth's voice became a whisper. "Keep thinking of the lake. You will feel something more in a moment. My mind will touch yours. Do not be afraid."

Faran did as he was told. He focused on the lake, and he found that the breathing exercise helped here. It enabled him to concentrate on one thing alone.

But his concentration wavered. Suddenly he felt Aranloth's mind slide over his own. It was like a glove going over a hand. It seemed to fit and it was comfortable, but it was disturbing at the same time.

Faran's focus on the lake wavered. Then it came back with incredible force. Suddenly nothing existed in the world but the lake, and he seemed to feel every drop as it moved and shifted in the great multitude of itself. He sensed also the two aspects of it. Deep below, where it was cold and dead, was elùgai. Up above, near the surface, where the light warmed it and the air touched it, was lòhrengai.

Halakness, Aranloth chanted. And Faran chanted it too. Although both seemed one. But he also sensed Ferla, and heard her voice also like a whisper in his mind.

Halakness. Their joined minds reached out and touched the lake. *Halakness.* The water seethed and shifted, towering up in a wave. Then the will of the lòhren let it go and withdrew.

Faran knew in that moment that Aranloth had sped their training by years. Through him, they had perceived a different world, and one that they could not have journeyed to on their own save by massive effort and time. But also, he sensed the urgency that drove the old man to do it. Everything they did now was for a purpose, and their skills would be tested before they were ready, no matter how well they trained.

17. A Thirst for Knowledge

Spring moved on to summer in the valley, and the broadleaf trees were dark with leaves while the grass sprang tall in the fields.

It grew quite hot during the days, and even the nights were warm. There were no windows in the back of the cabin where the bedrooms were positioned, and the room Faran shared with Ferla was hot and stuffy. Often, they sat together on one of the various benches or log seats outside well into the evening until it cooled down.

The garden out back prospered, and vegetables thrived in the good conditions. This was due to the soil, but mostly to the water applied to them frequently from the well.

Sometimes Aranloth, his broken arm from the battle in the tombs now healed, had them walk to the lake with buckets in order to retrieve water from the garden. Then he bade them do it running. This built stamina and balance he said, for if they spilled too much water he sent them back to refill again.

Nor was that the only running. A warrior might be called upon to fight for hours, he told them. And he set them destinations and timed them with a sandglass from the cabin. He expected an improvement every week.

Sometimes those runs were sprints. Here, Faran outpaced Ferla. But when Aranloth told them to run to the dead oak at the north crest of the valley, or the even longer distance to the beehive on the western rim, Ferla beat him home.

Aranloth did not limit their exercise regime to running alone. He showed them various types of squats, two and one legged, to build lower body strength. For the upper body, he showed them the ancient hedgehog pushup, as he called it, with the hands and elbows close together and the body arcing down and then up. These Faran found hard, and once again Ferla beat him at that.

But when it came to lifting large rocks from the ground and hurling them with both hands, Faran excelled there. This, the lòhren told them, trained all the muscles of the body to work in unison. For a warrior, he insisted, did not rely on strength of arm to wield a sword. It was the body that provided the strength, and the arm was an extension of that. So too, the sword was an extension of the arm.

Yet it was the sword forms that were the pinnacle of their physical training. Sometimes Aranloth would summon the illusion of the greatest warriors, not to spar, but just to demonstrate techniques. When he did this, he would have them stand behind the illusion and copy their movements.

Sometimes he did this slowly. Sometimes with speed they could not follow, but at least then they saw what was possible and what their goal was.

Brand was his favorite to follow. The man moved with a grace and intensity that was magical. Yet it was not magic but practiced skill, and that gave Faran hope that one day he could approach such attainment himself, if he only trained hard enough.

And copying the movements of these legends, both he and Ferla got better. Aranloth told them the names of new forms, and there were many of these. Nor did each of their summoned demonstrators perform the same movements in an identical fashion.

"They have made the move their own," Aranloth had told them. "These sword forms are not immutable. If your reach is longer or shorter, if you prefer a move for defense or for attack, if you are wide across the shoulders or narrower, these and many other things will change the movements slightly. Over time, you too will make these alterations as you discover and test the limits of your body."

Sometimes, there was no summoned illusion at all. Aranloth would call the names of sword forms in quick succession, and they would play them out at full speed as though in combat.

"Clouds Drift Across the Moon!" he would call. "Now Wolf in Tall Grass!" and on it went, one form blending into another.

And as the forms blended into one another, so too did the days of training blend into months. Faran grew stronger and fitter. His skill in body and mind ever increased.

It seemed to him that there were no limits to knowledge, and though he progressed more slowly than Ferla, still he moved ahead. And though he loved the physical training, it was the mental aspect that he liked the most. The sharpening of his will and the slow growth of magic that Aranloth had woken in him.

In this he excelled and outpaced Ferla just as she outpaced him with swordplay. But they each learned to calm their mind and summon magic with the aid of the words of power. Of those, Aranloth taught them many.

There were times that Faran knew he was far, far behind the training of his enemies who were knights. But he knew also that Aranloth did not hold back his knowledge. He taught when they were able to learn, and he enhanced their learning by overlaying his mind on theirs. This, he told them, was not a thing that he had ever done with the knights. It was the way of lòhrens instead, and Faran wondered if the old man taught them more magic than ever he had with the knights. He hoped so, for the disadvantage of time must be made up somehow.

One afternoon, as the long shadows from the trees up along the west ridge ran down the slopes, Aranloth had them spar each other. This they had done before, but never when one was blindfolded and the other not.

Ferla wore the blindfold, and though they both wore their armor, for this exercise they used only wooden practice swords.

What was strange to Faran was how often Ferla anticipated his moves and blocked a strike. She did not always do so, but it happened far more often than he thought chance should allow.

"Listen to the sound of his stepping," Aranloth had advised. Shortly after he instructed her to listen to her opponent's breathing. A sudden intake of breath might indicate an attack.

Faran knew all this was true, but he felt there was more going on. And then he had it. Ferla was also able to anticipate him because she knew what sword forms he favored and when he might most be inclined to use them.

This got him thinking. As always, Aranloth's training was two sided. It was not just for Ferla's benefit, but his own. If she could anticipate his moves to some degree when blindfolded, how much more so if she were not? Without knowing it, he followed patterns. And a skilled opponent could test and pry and discover those patterns in a fight. That was knowledge that might make the difference between life and death.

So it was that he understood unpredictability was an asset. Not just in a sword fight, but in any sort of conflict. From a blow to blow fight right through to the management of a military campaign involving multiple armies, the insight applied. Seek to discern your opponent's patterns, and seek to disrupt your own. Be intelligently erratic.

Their training continued as the weeks turned to months and high summer came and began to turn to the tail end of the year. Nuts and berries were in abundance, and the leaves of the trees lost their deep green hue and began to change.

It was Faran's favorite time of year. It was an ending that promised a new beginning to come. The cooler nights were soothing, and the still warm noontides comforting. It was a time to sit by the hearth and talk late into the night, and a time to be up early to feel the bite of upcoming winter snap at the air.

And always, no matter the season or the tasks of the day, their training continued apace.

Faran was happy here. Perhaps he was even happier here than he had been in Dromdruin. Aranloth was a hard teacher, but otherwise he was a kindly old man full of wisdom. Kareste did not involve herself in their training, but her loyalty to Aranloth was clear and she had risked her life for all of them. Her personality was the opposite of Aranloth's, and he enjoyed the direct way she had of speaking.

Then there was Ferla. He had been close to her in Dromdruin, but he was far closer now. Fate had bonded them together. He liked that closeness. He enjoyed it. And he wondered if she still thought of him like a younger brother. For though she acted to him like an older sister, he did not think that way about her at all.

There were times when he felt guilty though. How could he be happy? Dromdruin had fallen to swords and fire, and the men who did that, and the king who ordered it, walked free over the earth. But spilled blood called for justice, and murder for retribution. And he and Ferla were all that remembered Dromdruin, or cared, or that were in a position to seek that justice.

Or to try to seek justice, for how did one try to do that against a king, his knights, and the resources of a realm at their disposal?

These dark thoughts came and went. For the most part, he was happier than he had ever been in his life. A thirst for knowledge came to him as well. He had only ever experienced this before when he had learned how to hunt. But the pursuit of knowledge was like a hunt itself, and he delved deep into what Aranloth taught. Not just the ways of the body and how to use it, but the strengths of the mind. And magic most of all, which was wild as the lands that he loved to hunt.

The year grew old. The trees turned color and leaves fell, the sap in the trunks that gave them life slowing. Once-green grass was browned by leaves, and by the hard frosts that beautifully layered the land but killed. With the dying of the year, so too departed geese, swallows and hawks.

The land seemed to be holding its breath, waiting. But winter had not quite arrived. Yet one morning as Faran and Ferla returned from a long run, in their armor, having reached the beehive and finding it still, snow drifted from a clear sky to sting their faces as they ran.

The snowfall stopped by the time they reached the lower slopes. But coming back closer to the lake they saw a wagon before the cabin.

They knew that wagon, yet still they were cautious. They had seen no one else in all their time in the valley, but caution was now as much a part of their nature as it was with a wild deer picking its path through the trees.

They approached slowly and carefully, keeping to cover where they could. But it was to no avail.

A figure came out from the cabin and moved to the wagon to retrieve something. They sighed a little in relief. They had expected no one else, but being hunted sometimes made it hard to trust the very air they breathed.

Faran felt relief, and he looked forward to talking with the tinker. But he saw the look on the old man's face, and it was one of worry.

18. A Price in Gold

They sat at the sturdy table in the cottage. The hearth was warm, and breakfast was cooked. It was a feast this morning thanks to the arrival of the tinker. In the wild, when a traveler stopped by, the best food available was always put out.

Faran and Ferla still wore their armor. Jareck paid no attention to it, though it must have been a strange sight. Had he guessed who they were? Faran had no doubts.

They ate their meal in good humor, and the scent of smoke filled the room from the hearth. Nearby, sausages and slabs of meat hung for curing. It was a homely little place, but the tinker's expression was not encouraging.

When they were done, Faran and Ferla washed up, and the tinker passed on news of what was happening around Alithoras. Most of it seemed normal enough, but as they came back to the table to join the others his expression turned grim.

Leaning back in his chair, in the favored position reserved for guests closest to the warmth of the hearth, he filled and lit his pipe.

Aranloth broke the subject that loomed large within the small confines of the cabin.

"What news have you heard out of Faladir?"

Jareck puffed at his pipe. "I took your advice, old friend. I didn't go there. And well that I didn't, for even the news that reached me hundreds of miles away was bad enough."

He glanced at Faran and Ferla, and his eyes lingered on their armor.

"There's much talk of dark deeds and disturbances. It's said the king has become a tyrant. Fear breeds in the streets like shadows on a moonless night. Men go missing. Men who oppose the king. Some are found slain, perhaps the work of robbers. Perhaps not. Some men are never seen again."

Aranloth nodded. "It begins. But it will get worse."

"Oh, it already has," Jareck told him. "Rumor is, if you can believe it, that the king has used the Morleth Stone. It's said that lights often shine in the Tower of the Stone until the dawn brings the day to obscure it. It's also said that he sometimes takes the stone from the tower and walks among the people. They cower before him, and well they should. Rumor says he is a young man again, and that he tolerates no disobedience."

"I believe it," Aranloth whispered. "Yet it will get even worse yet. The stone will corrupt until nothing of humanity is left."

The tinker shivered and puffed deeply of his pipe, as though that perhaps might warm him.

"There's another rumor as well."

"Speak it," Aranloth told him.

"This one is only whispered, for it is death to say it to the wrong person."

Aranloth glanced at Ferla and Faran, then back to the tinker.

"Say it."

"You know what it is. You have known all along. What happens now in the streets of Faladir brings old tales to mind. The people speak of the founding of Faladir when the stone was raised against them first, and defeated. And they speak of the prophecy made when it was overcome and the Kingshield Knights first tasked with guarding it. One day they would fall. That has happened. And now the people whisper of the second part of that prophecy. They speak of the rising of the seventh knight, and they wonder where he is."

Faran felt guilt wash over him. The people were desperate for a hero, but it was not him. It would never be him, but that did not mean they were alone. When he had the skill to interfere in the enemy's plans, he would do so. What else could he do, in the meantime?

He looked at Ferla and saw that she had gone white. But her expression showed no fear, only determination.

Aranloth did not look surprised. "Druilgar will be doing all he can to stamp out that hope. There is more news yet to come, is there not?"

Jareck looked uncomfortable. "That there is. Worst news comes last, as they say." He took a deep breath. "You should know this. All your descriptions are circulated. All four of you. You are declared outlaws, and there is a price of gold on your heads. Anyone who can lead them to you will receive it. But the king does not wait on that alone. He has searchers out, including knights. They scour the countryside by day. At night, there is rumor of dark shadows that fly, seeking you also."

Again, Aranloth did not seem surprised. "It's a big land, Alithoras."

"It will need to be," Jareck muttered.

The conversation turned to other things then. It was clear that the old tinker knew exactly who they were, and he stood to gain much if he turned on them. But Aranloth trusted him, and there had been no point in his coming back here. Had he wanted to turn them in, he could have already done so. More than that, he had put himself at risk in coming here and warning them.

The tinker's presence did not put a stop to their training. After tending the garden, they went out by the lake with Aranloth and continued their practice. Jareck could hardly miss that, and if he had not guessed they were being trained as knights before, he would know it now beyond doubt.

It was a hard session. This time the lòhren summoned no illusory partner, but had them spar each other as they sometimes did. Nor did they use training swords, but their own blades.

Training with real weapons was different, and great care was needed. They had not started that way, but as they progressed Aranloth had insisted on it.

"The way you train is the way you fight," he had told them, and there was much truth in that. Facing a wooden sword was not the same as a steel blade that could kill. That changed how you moved and thought.

They circled each other now, Ferla's green eyes intent. She gave no warning of her strike, and like a viper's tongue the blade leaped toward his abdomen.

The tip of the blade nearly struck him. Perhaps it would have in a real fight, but she slowed to pull the blow at the last moment. His own sword clanged down against hers with a screech of steel, but that was not what saved him. It was his hasty retreat.

That was something he was working on. Retreat was all well and good, but it made it harder to deliver a return attack. Better to deflect an incoming blow and strike from where you stood. It eliminated that backward step and sped the return strike. That movement, albeit it only slightly faster, made all the difference. It put the opponent under pressure and caused them to retreat instead.

They circled again, and Faran dropped his weight and struck with The Swallow Dips Low, but Ferla moved back with the graceful counter of Serpent Recoils. From here, she was well positioned to spring back, but she was wary of him and remained at a distance. It was well for her, because he had only dropped low as a ploy to trick her into an attacking move she favored and that he was ready for.

It was probably no accident. She knew how he thought and what tactics he applied. Much of the time, she could read him like a book. She knew and understood him well. But he was not so good at reading her.

"That's enough for today," the lòhren called.

Faran and Ferla saluted each other. It was a sign of respect among the knights, but it also served to make a clear signal that the sparring session was over. It was a means of ensuring no accidents occurred.

They sheathed their blades and went to sit by Aranloth on the logs they favored. A cool breeze came off the lake, and Faran wondered if the waters froze in winter. Probably not. It was quite large, and they were farther south here and slightly warmer than Dromdruin had been.

"It troubles me," Faran said, "that Jareck could turn us in."

Aranloth considered that. "Do you think he will?"

"It's not that I think he will. I'm sure he won't. But he *could*. I might be wrong about him."

"That's always possible. Truth is though, sometimes you have to trust people. You just have to be discerning about it, and then once made let the decision go. Fear will make you doubt yourself. If you let it, it'll erode everything you believe and everything that you are."

Those seemed like wise words to Faran. They did not just apply to the situation with Jareck though. As always, the lòhren never wasted a moment to try to teach them something.

Aranloth was not done speaking. "You should also know this about the tinker. He's a man who has no use for gold, and never has. Better by far for him to travel the land he loves. He lives for that only, and nothing else. He's probably already rich, because he's been trading and tinkering for many, many years. But he cares nothing for that. He just wants to travel the land, far and wide, and he glories in the beauty of it."

There was a pause in the conversation for a good while after that. Ferla was the one to break it.

"Do the people really hope for the seventh knight to rise?"

Aranloth did not look at her. He kept his gaze far out over the lake, and his thoughts, whatever they were, could not be read. His face was a blank mask.

"Hope," he said at last, "is like the seeds of the earth. Drought may bake the land dry, but people still remember what green fields were like. And when it rains again, and even deserts know rain, they spring to life. Nothing can stop them."

Ferla nodded as though that was the very answer she expected.

They worked in the garden after that, and by evening had done yet another long run. After that, they swam in the lake as the long shadows crept down the slopes. Faran thought he saw a shadow among them, something that walked as a man, taking long strides, but even as he blinked and stared hard, he saw nothing more than the swaying shadows of a pine tree.

"What is it?" Ferla asked, drying her red hair on a towel.

"Nothing. I was just seeing things, but it's nothing."

She tossed the towel to him, and he dried his hair as well, but he kept looking again and again all along the slopes. Nothing was out of place, but he still felt uneasy. It was no more than the words of the tinker playing on his mind though.

Dinner was quiet, and the long night also. Faran did not sleep well, and when dawn came he was tired. But he and Ferla still did their early morning run, and returned in time to see Jareck off.

"I'll not come this way again until it's safe," the tinker told Aranloth. The lòhren had nodded at that and wished him well. Then the wagon rumbled forward. Even as it did, snow swirled in the air again, and a breeze came to life, cold as a knife.

19. Wards of Protection

A few days after the tinker had left, winter set in with a vengeance. The cold wind grew fiercer and fiercer, and then one night it snowed. And didn't stop all night.

Faran and Ferla did not run that morning. But they still donned their armor as usual, and they walked halfway up the western ridge. It was hard going, but the snow ceased and the sun rose, bathing them in warmer light. But it was still not warm. The power of the sun was weak, but they enjoyed it nonetheless.

"The valley looks so different," Ferla said.

"It's beautiful. But I'll enjoy a hot drink and some warm food inside the warmth of the cabin even more."

"Hush. I'd rather be here than anywhere else."

Faran gazed out over the valley, and he knew she was right. This was home now, and he loved it. Even if life was difficult.

There were no towns nearby, nor even villages. Nor would they go there if there were. Especially after the news the tinker brought. Whatever they ate, they had to hunt, gather or grow themselves.

But the garden prospered, and they had many vegetables that would store. Others could be dried or cured. The hunting and fishing had been excellent too. There was also an abundance of nuts, and these they cached in various places. That alone would see them survive. Even if the winter was harsh, they had food to see them through.

When they returned to the cabin, they did not go inside. The last of the garden needed harvesting, and this they did. By the time they finished, they were freezing. The metal of the armor drained all warmth from them, and their fingers were white and numb.

At length, they went inside and Kareste built up the fire. It did not warm them straight away, but over time they thawed out. A hot drink helped. It was some kind of tea, made of strong herbs and sweetened with honey from the beehive. Faran did not like it much, but it was warm, and Kareste told him the herbs were good for his health. He believed her, but he still did not like it.

"Where's Aranloth?" he asked.

"Gone for a walk," Kareste said. She could not quite hide the worry on her face. Aranloth had recovered after the tombs, but not fully. He still seemed weak, and she did not like the thought of him being alone out in the wild in this weather.

But the lòhren returned not long after, quickly shutting the door behind him to stop the rush of cold air that came with him.

Faran had seen the lòhren go out into the cold before, but it still amazed him that the old man wore only the clothes he always had and nothing further. He seemed immune to the cold, and perhaps that was some trick of magic. He and Ferla had taken to wearing deerskin cloaks.

The old man sat down by the hearth, and Kareste gave him the same tea that she had given the rest of them.

He took a sip, and then glanced at Faran and Ferla. "I haven't taught you yet the word of power for warmth, have I?"

Ferla groaned. "We could have done with that this morning. This armor is like ice."

"Hardship sharpens the mind," Aranloth answered. "Endurance of the woes of the world builds character."

"Be done with that knightly babble," Kareste said. "Just teach them how to do it."

Aranloth raised an eyebrow, but he did not answer her back.

"Think of the warmth in this room," he instructed. "Or if you are outside, when you will need this trick the most, think of the sun above. Or if at night, the slightly warmer air in a pocket of trees or coming off a west-facing cliff."

Faran thought of the warmth coming off the hearth. He felt it radiate through the air. He sensed the shifting and twining flames leap and dance above the burning wood. And underneath, he sensed the embers, hotter than the rest and steady.

"*Hrokhar*," intoned Aranloth. "Hrokhar, which is warmth. Feel the word. Feel the warmth. Know your mind, and understand that all three are one."

Faran almost had it. He uttered the word and sensed the power, but it slid from his grasp. Yet Aranloth's mind was there, slipping over his own, and then the warmth came. It was his to command.

When the lòhren withdrew his mind, that sense of control was gone. But Faran now knew what it felt like, and that he would be able to do it by himself at some point with more practice. Without the lòhren, such a thing might take years, if success ever came at all. With him, anything seemed possible.

Aranloth had shaved years off their training. Perhaps decades. Yet still the knights were well ahead of them, and the king held the Morleth Stone which granted him great powers. Perhaps he could do for the knights what Aranloth had just done.

They moved outside after that, the word of power fixed in their minds, and the cold did not seem as bad as it had before. Although that might just be the sun rising higher.

The lake had changed. It was still as it often was, but no ice had formed. Yet here and there where groves of willows grew along its banks, they had lost their leaves. Dead the trunks and branches seemed, and stark against the sky, but new life would flow into them when spring came. New life as had come to Faran, for he was not the same as he had been in Dromdruin.

They sat on an old tree trunk that had long ago fallen, and Faran knew what type of training would come next. Aranloth always took them here when he wanted to sharpen their minds rather than their sword skills.

"Tell me," the lòhren said, "the purpose of poetry."

They had conversed like this before, debating topics that at first had been well beyond Faran's grasp, but he had learned.

"Poetry is to entertain," he answered. "By the power of its beauty it seizes attention and uplifts the spirit."

Aranloth nodded. "What of you, Ferla. What answer do you give?"

Ferla looked away. "I don't know the answer. But must there be one true answer? Poetry may please you for one reason, and myself for another. Why should they not both be right?"

"Well, those are both good answers," Aranloth said.

Faran hesitated, and then spoke. "But which one is correct?"

The old man laughed. "I don't know. I lean toward Ferla's answer, but who is to say? You could have the right of it."

These sorts of conversations were often like this. Aranloth asked questions for which there was no answer. And in truth, Faran had begun to realize that he did not want one. What was more important here was the way they thought, and that their minds were opened to other views.

"The ways of the knights are deeper by far than skill at battle and magic alone. A knight can fight a creature of the shadow to the death, or dine with the queen and discuss the scrollwork on her favorite cutlery." He looked at them by turns. "So who will answer this first? Why does a bird have two wings and not one?"

Faran shook his head in amusement. Only a lòhren could ask such a question.

Ferla answered quickly though. "Because with one wing alone, how could a bird fly? It would be unbalanced, and would fly in a circle unable to go where it needed."

Faran knew the rules of this game well. His job was to come up with an alternative answer, and one that seemed plausible. That showed that he had considered the problem from different angles. But it was hard when Ferla gave what was obviously the correct answer.

"Well?" pressed Aranloth.

"Only a person would ask such a question. The bird just flies, and it needs no answer as to how it does what it does."

Aranloth clapped his hands together. "Very good! You're getting better at this." He turned to Ferla. "And what is the rebuttal to his answer?"

"Neither he nor I are birds. Birds may not question things, but people do. That is our nature just as much as it is the nature of birds to fly."

The lòhren seemed pleased with their answers, but he was not done.

"Now for a question that troubles the sharpest of minds. What is truth?"

Faran considered his response. He hated these elusive and vague questions, especially the ones that seemed to have such an obvious answer. But he had learned much about himself by trying to answer them well, and more by thinking on Ferla's responses, which were often far different from his own.

"Truth," he said, "is a fact. It can be proven by observation, experiment or testimony of reliable witnesses."

Ferla shook her head. "Who determines the reliability of witnesses? At best, that's only an estimate. And observation relies on interpretation of what is seen, which is as much as to say it's only an opinion. Nor is experimentation any different. In the end, the results must be interpreted just as observation is, and are therefore just as likely to be twisted by personal preference and prejudice."

Both points of view were plausible. Both could seem reasonable, and Faran knew from past experience that Aranloth would not choose one as correct over the other. Sometimes, he wished he would though.

"This brings us close to another question," the old man said. "Is perception reality?"

Faran knew he could get dizzy if he thought about these types of things too much, but Ferla grinned. She enjoyed the game.

"If you believe something to be true," she said, "then it's true. If you feel cold, then you *are* cold. If you're hot, then you *are* hot. If you're hungry, then you *are* hungry. It matters nothing that the person beside you may feel the opposite that you do. Perception is reality, and trying to filter reality through someone else's perception is like asking a bird to run and a deer to fly."

Faran looked out over the lake. A cold breeze blew ripples over its surface now and made his eyes water. But better to look there than at Ferla. If he did, she would distract him.

"If a person is sick, they may feel cold and shiver despite it being a warm day. Or a fever may wrack them, making them hot when in truth it's cool. Perception is therefore unreliable. Better to judge what is real by reference to past personal experience and the common perception of a group of people. This is less likely to be misleading."

They trained then for a little while in the magic that Aranloth was teaching them, and they learned new words of power. These new ones, just as with the old ones, they could not use to much effect by themselves, but with the lòhren's mind overshadowing their own, they progressed by slow increments.

So too had their sword craft. They fought Aranloth's summonings, and sometimes they won, and sometimes they lost, but they always learned.

And they sparred each other also. This was often with practice swords, but they had moved on as well to a kind of slow sparring with their own blades. It was here most of all that Ferla came alive, and often she grinned for sheer joy as they fought. This was a habit that Aranloth was trying hard to break her from.

It was cold again by evening, colder than it had been all year. A pale moon rose, full and bright in the clear sky. They ate their dinner and then gathered close to the hearth. Glad was Faran for all the timber he and Ferla had cut through the summer, but Aranloth seemed troubled, and he held tightly to his staff.

"Something comes," he said after a little while. "Something evil. I feel it in my bones."

Kareste seemed worried, and she too held her staff tightly. But she said nothing, merely moving to the door and opening it, but not stepping outside.

The others joined her, each looking out the door. But there was nothing to see but the rising moon and the creeping shadows over the valley slopes.

"There," hissed Aranloth, and he pointed with his staff.

Something moved down by the lake, but it sought no cover nor tried to hold still to hide itself. Instead, it strode toward them.

Faran felt a sense of dread build. The figure was alone, but menace came from it. It walked through their training ground where they practiced, and that felt like a violation to him. How dare this thing come here and seek them out?

For seek them out it did. It strode toward them, sure of purpose, and as it did so it became clearer. Tall it was, dressed in robes of black, and a staff was in its hand.

"Is it an elùgroth?" Ferla asked, and Faran was impressed with the calmness of her voice.

"No," Aranloth answered. "It is worse. It is impossible, yet there it stands before us."

Faran knew then. It was the thing that hounded them. It had hunted them since the standing stones. It had pursued them through the tombs of the Letharn, and survived and escaped both Aranloth and the harakgar. It was the shadow.

Yet in the silvery light of the moon, the thing cast a shadow itself. It had grown. It had become solid. It was less a shadow now than a person, but how was such transformation possible?

The shadow-creature drew up before the cabin. Regal it was, in a dark way. A thing of great power. If it were a man, it would surely be some great lord. But it was no man.

Yet still it spoke, and its voice was both strange and familiar.

"Come forth, lòhren. You and I must battle this night. I can abide you no longer."

Faran looked to Aranloth. He knew the creature spoke to him and not Kareste. But it was Kareste who acted. With a swift move, she closed the door and barred it.

Silence fell, deep and heavy. When Faran spoke, he hoped for Ferla's calm, but his voice was high, and trembly.

"The door will not keep it out,"

"No," Kareste answered. "But Aranloth and I have not been idle. We have cast wards of protection over this building. That magic is stronger than timber."

Faran and Ferla drew their swords. No noise came from without, nor any sign of the shadow.

"It will not work," Aranloth said softly to Kareste. "Our wards are set to defy the dark magic of the stone, but this is something else."

"They'll still hold. And if they don't, then we fight."

He shook his head. "I don't think so. Whatever this thing is, it is for me to fight and no other. I feel the truth of that. I have always felt the truth of that."

At that moment there was a roar of noise and something smashed against the door. There was a wave of heat, and Faran knew the creature had struck at them with flame. Yet around its edges, which he saw through the windows, was a flickering movement of blackness. Just as the creature was of shadow, so too the flame it summoned.

The door held. Had it not been protected by magic, Faran knew even the heavy oak panels would have sundered to shards and embers.

"The wards need strengthening," Kareste said. She looked at Faran and Ferla. "You must help. There is a word of power for this. *Haeldurn*. It means protect. Say it, and think of the cabin as a shell around you, made invulnerable by magic."

They began to chant. Outside, more of that black light flared and the door rattled on its hinges.

"Haeldurn," Faran chanted. And Ferla did likewise beside him. He saw both Aranloth and Kareste take on an appearance of concentration, but they said no words. Yet still, he sensed their power spring to life and feed the wards that he now sensed all around them.

But he understood those wards now that he had sensed them with his mind. They repelled magic. They would do nothing against normal forces. But there *was* a normal force the creature might use against them. Fire. Not fire born of magic, but just plain fire.

The creature must realize that too. It must be able to sense the wards, but it had not taken that next step. Why would that be?

Faran turned to the old man. "This thing doesn't want to kill you. It wants you alive. It wants to fight you, but not kill you."

20. A Duel of Magic

Once more, the door rattled and a dull boom sounded as though of thunder. This time, the whole cabin shook.

Faran concentrated on the chant, and whatever power he had, so little and weak as it seemed to him, he felt it join to the great swelling of magic from the others. The wards flared to brighter life, and they held timber together that would long since have broken and blown apart under the strain of the assault they endured.

The shadow ceased to throw fire at them. Now, a wind rose, and it howled in from a distance and then reached the cabin. The walls, made of logs as they were, still swayed. The roof jolted. The roar of the wind was deafening. Without the wards, the cabin would have been picked up and cast away. Yet it held.

Faran chanted. He gave everything he had, his mind focused on the concept of Haeldurn, of protection. The wards had been weakened by the attack, but they strengthened again now. Yet they were not as strong as they were.

Then a new attack came, the wind seemed to scream at them, and then it died away to a whimper and was gone. A profound silence grew. Even the silence seemed loud. It was as though Faran could feel it as an actual force.

"The creature has used fire and wind against us," Aranloth whispered into the silence. "Now it uses the weight of air. It piles it upon us, and it buttresses it from the sides."

"But air weighs nothing," Faran said.

"Its weight is very small," Aranloth told him. "But it adds up. And there is no limit to it."

Faran went back to chanting the word of power, and he forced his will into that word and made it one with the wards. Yet still the pressure grew, and it seemed that a weight of mountains was upon him, and the logs of the cabin groaned.

But the wards held, and the pressure released suddenly with a long rolling boom.

"Come out and face me as you must in the end," the creature called. And it spoke in a voice like Aranloth's own, mocking him.

"Do not even think about it, old man," Kareste said.

Aranloth straightened. "I must. This thing has dogged me, whatever it is. It will not give up. It must be defeated."

"We can escape," Kareste argued.

Faran did not see how. There was no way out of here except past the thing that attacked them.

"To what end?" Aranloth asked. "It will find me again. Somehow we are joined, and it will shadow me across all the world if I run. No. I will not do it, and it weakens me to do so. I am not what I was, nor as strong as I should be. Better to fight now and have an end to it."

Kareste took a firm grip of her staff. "Then we will confront it together."

"No. I will not allow that," Aranloth said. "You have another duty, and a greater. If necessary, escape with Faran and Ferla. Teach them what I would have taught them."

With that, he reached for the door and opened it. The silvery light of the moon spilled into the room.

"I come, my shadow," Aranloth said.

The tall figure outside leaned on its staff. "You have it wrong, lòhren. You are *my* shadow."

That made no sense to Faran, but he stood in the doorframe, Kareste and Ferla either side of him.

The two figures circled one another, and in truth, they did look like shadows, for they matched each other move for move.

And then the duel continued that had begun months ago on the bridge of stone in the tombs of the Letharn.

The shadow struck first, pointing its staff and hurling shadow-fire at Aranloth. The lòhren made no move to evade it. Instead, he raised his arms as though to embrace it. The dark magic struck him, but he seemed to absorb it, and then fling it back at his opponent. As it returned, the blackness was shot through with swirling strands of silver.

The shadow leaped away, moving fast and flinging up shadows all around it to obscure exactly where it stood.

The pale moonlight danced and jerked over the snow-covered earth, and Aranloth's opponent blended in with all those shifting lights.

Aranloth did not stand still. He leaped forward, light flaring from the tip of his staff. This revealed the dark thing, crouched low to one side. But it was not cowering there. Rather it was buying time for its next attack.

And that attack came with a roar of wind that sent leaves hurling before it, and a moment later a driving wall of snow. Now, instead of shadows, the scene before the cabin was white. Snow rolled over the ground. Snow filled the air and enveloped the lòhren, then it tightened and coalesced into ice.

Faran held his breath. These opponents seemed perfectly matched, and he wondered how that was possible. Surely one should have an edge over the other. He also knew he witnessed a battle such as few alive had ever seen. The forces of magic were stupendous, and the skill and long years of training that had developed it were beyond his comprehension. It would take many lives of men to reach such power, and he knew that if he trained the rest of his life his talents would be as a drop of water in a lake compared to this.

Aranloth seemed frozen, and icicles hung from his jawline like a beard. But he cried out, and the light of the moon intensified, shining for a moment like the sun, and it filled the little area of the combat, swirling like the snow had done.

Faran felt warmth from it, but it would be most intense near the lòhren, and even as he looked at the old man he saw the ice turn to steam and lift into the air.

The creature of shadow cursed in some foreign tongue. Aranloth exalted in another. What they said Faran could not understand, but he sensed the emotions behind their strange words.

The two combatants paused, each leaning on their staff and gazing at each other. Like twins they were, only Aranloth's face was clear, but his opponent wore a hood that shadowed his.

But suddenly Aranloth moved, raising high his staff and then pulling it back. His opponent crouched in a defensive position, but then slowly straightened as nothing happened.

"You weaken, Aranloth. And soon you will be mine."

Aranloth did not answer, but he backed both away and stepped to the side. The shadow made to move toward him, but then paused mid-stride and looked behind him.

Faran had seen it before him. Aranloth had summoned a great towering wave of water from the lake. It rolled up from the shore, higher than the cabin, growing as it came until it stretched high as a tree.

The water was dark in the moonlight, but the foamy crest of the wave glowed silver. Then it blocked out both moon and sky and fell crashing atop the shadow.

Water surged everywhere, smashing into the cabin but repelled by the wards.

Aranloth stood tall. Water swirled and foamed around him, but he was as an island amid the tumultuous sea.

Of the shadow, there was no sign, and Faran doubted anything could have survived that wall of water. Or if not killed, at least it would be cast down.

Yet as the water receded, the dark shadow was revealed. It stood there just as Aranloth, untouched by the water and seemingly master of its environment. Aranloth gave no sign of surprise, but Kareste drew a sharp breath.

The two combatants surveyed each other, hatred in the posture of one and puzzlement in the other. They were equally matched, and the one could gain no advantage over the other…

Faran understood something of what was happening then, and made his choice.

"Aranloth cannot win," he said. "He is fighting himself. The shadow *is* him, some shadow of him born from the void."

Kareste did not answer. She frowned, and then realization dawned on her face. Faran was right, and seeing that, he leaped into action.

With a wild cry he dashed from the cabin and ran at the shadow. His sword gleamed palely in the moonlight, and then he felt something within it stir to life. The magic that he had been told was there but never felt till now, woke.

The sword caught alight with a cold blue flame, and Faran attacked the shadow. He swung high, aiming a blow that would decapitate the enemy, then dropped swiftly low. The first movement was a ploy, and the second the real attack.

But the shadow was fast. Or else it knew the move even as Aranloth did. With contempt, it flicked its staff to deflect the blow and then swung it back to strike Faran across the head.

It was the helm that saved him. It absorbed the blow, though it rang like a bell, yet the magic in it flared as well and repelled the stream of shadow-fire that erupted from the staff's tip.

Faran fell back. But Kareste and Ferla were there, launching their own attacks. If not for them, he did not think the magic of the armor would have saved him for long.

He scrambled upright, sword raised high, and yelled at Aranloth.

"Remember the words of the queen! You are your own enemy! The shadow is *you*!"

Kareste leveled her staff and lòhren-fire leaped from its tip. The shadow swayed out of the way, then sent a blast of dark magic at her that sent her sprawling. Ferla darted forward, her blade sweeping through the air in Tempest Blows the Dust, but the shadow flung black flame at her and she tumbled away, her armor smoking.

Then suddenly Aranloth was there, and resolution was on his face.

"I know you now, creature. And I name you. You are Aranloth. You are the worst of Aranloth, all the things that I suppress. You are my dark side, my shadow in truth. But I know you now."

The shadow recoiled. "You cannot defeat me!"

Aranloth leaned on his staff. "No. I cannot defeat you, for we are one. Two aspects of the same thing, like the sun and the moon. But you are a part of me. I need not defeat you. I merely acknowledge you. You are my dark side, and I know you now. You are the voice of hatred and despair, of jealousy and greed. You are cowardice and pride. You are all these things, and you are also a shadow. You are the lesser me. Equal in power, but of no value to the world."

"No! I am the master! *You* are the shadow!"

"It is not so. It was never so, through all the long years of my life. I know you. I name you Aranloth. You are *me*!"

The lòhren opened his arms, and a silvery nimbus glowed around him. The shadow shrunk. Its staff fell from its hands, but when Faran looked there was nothing on the snow.

Aranloth stepped toward the shadow, and the white light that came from him shone over it and enveloped it. Then he shuddered and fell to one knee, using his staff to keep him upright.

"It is done," he whispered.

21. What Went Wrong

Aranloth sat on his favorite log seat by the lake. Faran and Ferla were with him, and Faran could not quite believe how much the old man had changed since last night.

The weakness and frailty that had beset him since Traveling was gone. He was his old self. Strong, confident and with a sense of great power swirling below a tranquil exterior.

In one respect, he had changed from his old self though. At least for this morning. He was talkative and in the mood to answer questions.

They had asked him about the shadow, and he had been free with his responses.

"It was a combination of magics that gave life to it, I believe," he said. "Traveling is a dangerous thing. Too dangerous by far except under dire circumstances. Even then, maybe it's best left alone. There are powers and forces at work in the void beyond human understanding." The old man shook his head. "Perhaps I should not have ventured it, but what is done is done."

Faran was not so sure about that. If they had not Traveled, then Lindercroft would have had them.

"Then there was my own lòhrengai, and the summoning of the king," Aranloth went on. "Three powerful magics bound together and hurtled through the void. Anything could have happened, and perhaps we can be grateful that some evil far worse was not unleashed upon the world."

"But was the shadow really you?" Ferla asked.

"Indeed it was, and Faran was right. The dark calls to the dark, and all those forces together in the void called to the dark side of my nature and drew it from me."

"Do we all have such a dark side?" Faran asked.

"All of us. And this is part of your training. At least, it's part of the training of a Kingshield Knight. The human spirit is a blend of good and bad. Temptation is always with us. Self-interest. Jealousy. Greed. They are a part of us, and the more you pretend they don't exist, the greater the chance they can hold sway over you. A knight acknowledges the dark side to their nature, and strives to overcome it. If a person is unaware of that battle going on inside them, then how can they win the fight?"

They talked a little while longer. More and more their training had become philosophical. But they did not neglect the martial aspects. Soon, they began to spar again.

Ferla grinned as they circled each other, but she did not attack this time. Often she was the more aggressive of the two, forcing Faran to defend. But not today.

He realized she was changing her tactics so as not to become predictable. He could have waited her out if he wanted, for he was sure that if he did not attack her instincts would win out and she would attack him. But it was time that he bettered this aspect of his skills. It was easier to defend than attack, but there were situations that demanded attack and swift resolution of a fight. He had to improve at that.

He drove forward, sending the point of his blade toward her abdomen and at an upward angle. It was a strike better suited to someone who did not wear armor, for if successful it penetrated flesh and then pierced the heart. Yet even with armor it could cause great pain. And there were times also when a good sword could drive through poor quality or damaged armor.

Ferla reacted quickly to his move though. She retreated into Serpent Recoils, and even as he began to withdraw she leaped upon him with a strike of the side of her sword against his helm.

It was a heavy blow, stronger than she intended, and Faran staggered back. Ferla hesitated, watching to see if he was alright.

"Enough," Aranloth called. He pointed his staff at Ferla. "You did well, and I understand your concern. But never hesitate. As you train so will you fight. To hesitate now is to train your instincts to momentarily pause in a battle. If that happens, the advantage you gained might be lost beyond recall."

Faran took off his helm and shook his head. He was glad that she had not followed up despite what Aranloth had said. But he knew the old man was right.

His head still rang, and when he looked at Ferla he saw she had a small grin on her face. That was just adding insult to injury. She enjoyed beating him, but after a brief feeling of frustration he found he did not mind. She would always be the better sword fighter. He could live with that, but his skill in magic surpassed hers, and likely always would. That just made them stronger when they were together.

Kareste walked down the side of the lake to join them. The shore was disturbed from the fight last night, and she used her staff to help her walk over the wetted ground where Aranloth had called up the water to attack the shadow.

Faran was intrigued. Kareste never interrupted their training, but there was no urgency in the way she walked toward them so nothing important had happened that she had to tell them.

"How goes the training?" she asked when she reached them.

"It progresses," Aranloth answered. "I'll make warriors of them yet."

Kareste looked them over. "Maybe. They have the courage of warriors – that they have shown a number of times, not least last night." She flicked the end of her staff with her foot and raised it before her as a weapon. "But let's see how they spar."

She approached Faran, but he backed away. "I have a sword, Kareste. A staff is no match for that."

She merely laughed. "Do you think so? Then let me educate you."

She thrust the staff at him, using it like a spear rather than the staffs he had seen used in Dromdruin.

He backed away and lifted high his sword. If she wanted to spar, then spar they would. He made to step forward and attack, but she beat him to the move, knocking the sword sideways and striking against his helm with a flick of the staff point. Then she danced away, out of reach.

Looking into her eyes, he saw that she was not like Ferla at all. There was no grin there, but only an implacable will backed by supreme confidence in her skill. That, and how easily she had just hit him convinced him to take this seriously. He had been wrong not to do so. Very wrong. There was something to learn here.

He darted forward in Running Hare Changes Course. It was a technique he was good at, but it availed him nothing here. Kareste glided back as he came forward, deflected his blade and struck him across the helm again.

But he did not give up the attack. He moved immediately into The Swallow Dips Low, trying to edge forward and catch her with a surprise strike at the legs.

It did not work. This time her staff crashed down straight on top of his helm knocking him to the ground, and when he rolled to the side, swaying up in Fish Swims

Upright, her staff found a gap in his defenses and struck him with the tip in his belly and winded him.

"Enough, I think," Aranloth called. "He has learned that the staff can beat the sword."

"That I have," Faran said. He gave Kareste a bow. "This has given me much to think about."

"The chief lesson is this," Aranloth said. "A staff has greater reach, at least when used like a spear as Kareste just did. It has no cutting edge, nor the weight of metal, so in many ways is less dangerous. Yet the greater reach is an advantage, and the tip of the staff is dangerous. Very dangerous, for it can knock a warrior out. Then even the smallest of daggers can kill him."

Kareste glanced at Ferla. "Your turn, now. Let's see if you can do better than Faran did."

Faran was glad to see that she did not. Then he felt bad that he was glad. Yet Ferla did get better as the sparring continued, and once toward the end she got past the dangerous point of the staff and in close where her sword could be used to effect. Only Kareste was able to dart backward quickly enough to avoid it, and they were back where they had begun.

Aranloth called a halt to the unusual sparring session soon after.

"I'll cut a staff for you later so that this can become part of your training. And I'll teach you how to use it as a weapon in its own right, and how to counter it when you carry a sword. But that will just be the beginning. Your training will also encompass daggers, and throwing knives, maces, halberds and spears. For your enemies may use all of these things."

"What about bows and arrows?" Ferla asked with a cheeky grin.

"That you already have great skill in," Aranloth answered. "But I'll teach you about bows that you're not familiar with, such as the cavalry bow and how it's used in battle."

Though they trained hard, they had chores to do also. The garden was not in use now, due to the cold, but they had a harvest of vegetables that needed checking in the shed. The root harvest needed sorting onto wooden racks so it had air circulating and rot was less likely. And those that were damaged, and likely to rot, removed from the others and taken to the cabin for sooner use.

There was a harvest of apples that needed treating in similar fashion. These had come from a tree they had discovered well behind the cabin. Grass and weeds had grown around it, and several bushes half covered it, but it had responded well when they cleared the choking mess away and hauled water to it through the hot days of summer.

Some of their chores done for the day, they went on one of their runs. The ground was treacherously wet, for much of the snow had melted, but it still lay thick in sheltered hollows and the valley remained beautiful. It seemed no great labor to run to one of the ridges now, even in armor, and this time they went to the dead oak on the northern crest of the valley.

There they sat a while and rested, their backs to the great trunk, and looked down on their home.

"I love it here," Ferla said.

Faran glanced at her. There was a hint of a grin on her face like when they sparred. He knew she meant the words, and there was a light in her eyes as she looked across the valley from one end to the other.

"I love it too," he said. "I could be happy here. I mean, I *am* happy here. But I would also be happy to spend the rest of my life here."

She leaned against him then, shoulder to shoulder, but they said no more.

They both knew that sooner or later their stay here would come to an end. The burning of Dromdruin still required justice. But they did not speak of that. It would destroy the mood, and they had both learned the value of enjoying what was good while it lasted.

22. The Strategies of War

Winter hardened its grip on the land. In the valley, the snow lay deep in the low places and the edges of the lake were frozen. Wolves howled at night, hunting for scarce food, and small birds died of cold where they perched on branches hung with icicles.

The days were bad, and the nights were worse. In the silent marches of darkness, while the occupants of the cabin slept, occasionally a mighty crack sounded and shattered the stillness as tree trunks were split by swelling sap.

Sometimes the air was hard to breathe, for it burned the lungs like fire. And to wear armor outdoors for long was to court death.

Yet the training of Faran and Ferla continued in this harsher winter than they expected. It was mostly done now in the cabin, and the fire burned day and night in the hearth. It was cozy inside, if cramped. They practiced sword forms even here, one at a time, but they did not spar.

More and more their training changed. They delved deeper into magic, and they also learned the strategies of war.

Long into the night, Aranloth would tell them of battles, ancient and recent, and of the leaders of armies and the choices they made. And why. He told them of victories and defeats. He told them of victories that had been grasped from the jaws of defeat, and losses that were unthinkable.

He told them why these things had happened. And later, he told the stories and asked for opinions as to what had been a good strategy and what a bad before he told them the final outcome.

In this way they learned a great deal of the history of Alithoras. Yet also they learned military strategy and how commanders thought and acted.

One night they sat before the fire. Outside, a storm raged and wind howled. Against the northern side of the cabin, the snow piled deep and even the fire seemed to barely provide protection against the relentless cold.

"If the enemy outnumbers you, what do you do?" Aranloth asked.

As always, he held his staff close, but his hands were white from cold as he spoke. Faran and Ferla had long since wrapped themselves in blankets and sat on their hands to keep them warm.

"Never directly engage with a superior opponent," Faran answered. "Not unless there is a means to negate their advantage and gain superiority yourself."

Aranloth nodded. "And what means must be looked for to reverse a disadvantage of numbers?"

"Superior terrain on which to fight. Or an advantage of equipment, fighting skill or leadership."

Aranloth sat back. "Is there anything you would add to that, Ferla?"

"The morale of the opponent is also a factor. How well will they fight? Are they fighting for a cause they believe in? Does their leadership inspire them?"

"All good points," Aranloth said. "In war, numbers are not everything. *Winning* is everything. Fight only when you are more likely to do that than your enemy. Be sure of this before you commit."

In the hearth, a small log popped with a flare of smoke and shifted. Kareste added another one to the fire. It remained cold in the cabin.

"What is the purpose of scouts?" Aranloth asked.

"Knowledge is power," Ferla answered straight away. "To know the terrain, enemy movements, food sources, allies or other enemies likely to be encountered is critical to good decision-making."

"Do you have anything to add, Faran."

"No, Osahka." It felt a little strange for him to use that title, but he was getting more used to it. "Knowledge is a tool as much as swords or bows. Even more so, because it enables these other tools of warfare to be used to best advantage. And to avoid surprises. This is the true enemy of a general."

Outside, the wind howled even louder, but at last some warmth from the fire seemed to be building up inside the cottage.

Aranloth rubbed his hands together and blew on them, as though suddenly surprised that it had been cold.

"And how is truth used in military strategy?" he asked.

Ferla grinned. "Only as a means of deceiving the enemy."

The old man turned to Faran. "Give me an example."

Faran thought about all the battles Aranloth had told them of, and he found one that provided a good example.

"During the Shadowed Wars, King Gaeblung used truth effectively as a means of deceit. His army was low on supplies and had many wounded from previous battles. He was in no position to engage a superior force, yet was faced with one that he could not outmaneuver. His army was infantry, while the enemy was cavalry. So he allowed enemy scouts to observe his weaknesses. Then he fled. The enemy, knowing his weakness and believing the flight real, attacked. But it was a ruse and Gaeblung turned to attack in his turn, but only after he had lured the cavalry into charging uphill against his ranks of battle-hardened pikemen. He won the field, and his archers came in from the wings to destroy the enemy."

Aranloth looked pleased. "So you listen to my stories after all. Not only that, you learn from them. I'm impressed."

Faran felt good. Praise from the lòhren was not exactly rare, but it did have to be earned.

"Answer me this," Aranloth continued. "When should the commander of an army fight the enemy in person?"

Ferla gave answer quicker than Faran. It was often a competition between them.

"A commander must balance many things," she replied. "The army loves to see the commander fight. It strengthens morale. But it comes with great peril. To fight is to risk death, and should the commander be killed the army may be routed. So the commander should fight only when absolutely necessary. For instance, to bolster a line the enemy is near to breaking, and that if they do, will win them the field."

Aranloth turned to Faran. "What do you say?"

Faran did not answer at once. He thought deeply, for though Aranloth had described many battles to them, no two battles were identical. There was never a single perfect answer.

"I say what Ferla does. But determining when it's necessary or not is not so simple. Once a line breaks, it may be too late to fix it. So a commander may have to err on the side of caution. They may need to fight and strengthen morale *before* it is clear the line will break. To wait until certainty is to wait too long." He paused and thought some more. "There is also this. A commander must spare thought for the future. He, or she, must build their reputation for courage, luck and good decisions under extreme pressure. They must prove themselves to the soldiers who follow, and in this way they can lead by example. Soldiers learn to fight *for* their commander then, and to believe in them. In this way the morale of the army can be heightened. And one way to achieve this is to risk combat even when unnecessary. A risk now may plant the seed of future success."

Aranloth pursed his lips. "An interesting strategy. Yes, very interesting. I fear few commanders would agree with you. But the greatest of them probably would. The greatest of them are capable of taking the greatest risks, but they do so only rarely and when great gain is possible."

Kareste stirred. "Brand was one such. He took enormous risks, but he seemed to know by instinct when it was time to do so. At other times, he was extremely cautious."

Aranloth nodded. "There are few like him, though. But speaking of great leaders, how can you tell if the enemy general is incompetent instead?"

Faran answered first this time. "That is something that you cannot tell – not with certainty. The enemy may truly be incompetent. Or they may be deceiving you into believing so in order to encourage you into misstepping. It is best to at all times to assume the enemy is skilled."

"So it is indeed," Aranloth replied. "Now, someone tell me the different kinds of warfare."

Ferla beat him to answering here, but Faran did not mind. Her answers were always good, and he enjoyed the sound of her voice.

"The first kind is to attack with superior numbers, or other advantages, when victory is most assured."

"But the opposite of that," Faran added, "is to retreat or evade, with inferior numbers, seeking an opportunity to gain the advantage."

The old man put another piece of wood in the fire. At last it was growing warm in the cabin, but the storm outside only grew in ferocity, and the valley must be deep in snow by now.

"What other kinds are there," Aranloth asked.

"To deprive the enemy of food, supplies or morale. This is an indirect means of war," Faran answered, "best used to attain a slow victory when a direct attack will not yield one."

Faran was pleased with his answer. He knew his knowledge of war was superficial. How could it be otherwise? He had never fought in an army, still less directed a battle. Yet Aranloth was a good teacher, and the training he gave prepared for both. So while there was much yet to be learned, he had still learned a great deal. He was *not* the same person that he had been less than a year ago. Nor was Ferla.

Aranloth settled back in his chair, but his eyes remained alert.

"One last question tonight," he said. "What are the reasons given for making war?"

Neither Faran nor Ferla answered. They looked at each other, somewhat perplexed. This was not a direction that their conversations had gone in before.

"To defeat enemies," Faran said.

"A simple answer," Aranloth said. "But not an inaccurate one. What of you, Ferla?"

"War is an extension of diplomacy by steel rather than words."

Faran remembered the old man saying that once before, but he could not recall if he had agreed with it, or merely mentioned it.

"That too," Aranloth said, "is a simple answer, but likewise not an inaccurate one." He leaned forward now, his voice nearly drowned out by the howling wind outside.

"Those are reasons given for war. But tell me its *true* purpose?"

Faran thought deeply. "The purpose of war is to create peace when other means have failed."

Ferla tilted her head to the side. "I'm not sure. It may be as Faran says. Or it may be that it is in the nature of humanity to unleash its dark side. Just as it is in the nature of a bird to fly or a fish to swim.

The wind moaned outside, and the cabin rattled. Faran hoped his answer was right, but he feared Ferla was correct.

23. All Things End

Winter gripped the valley hard, but here and there were warmer days that saw Faran and Ferla continue their training. Even in the snow, they walked to the ridges and back to the cabin. So too their sword lessons continued, and added to them was training with staff and knife.

When it was too cold outside, they trained inside. This was difficult, and they could not spar, but they could refine their techniques under Aranloth's watchful gaze.

But bit by bit, winter loosed its grip. Spring came, and the thaw with it. The lake rose high in its basin, and many little creeks and springs flowed through the valley. Birds that had migrated began to return, and though there were still some days of bitter cold there were also ones of blue sky and beautiful sunlight.

The garden needed digging over, and this they did in preparation for the spring and summer crops to come. This was hard work, but both Faran and Ferla had grown strong, and they tackled it with enthusiasm.

Their stores of food were lower, but they still hunted well and cured more meat. And fish, as always, were plentiful in the lake.

One fine morning, they trained in their favorite place by the water's edge, close to where they often fished. The sun shone, and it was the warmest day so far.

Aranloth had conjured one of his illusory warriors, and Faran faced him. But this was no ordinary warrior. It was a Kingshield Knight, and this was something the lòhren had not done before.

But Faran was confident. He had trained hard. His sword was of the same quality as his opponent's, as was his armor. The knight, whoever he was or had been, for Aranloth often conjured the images of warriors long dead, was more experienced than him. But Faran felt young and strong, and increasingly he knew he had attained skill.

The knight glanced at him with cool eyes. They were eyes that had seen fights before, but there was great intelligence there also. But those eyes gave no foreshadowing of the attack to come.

In one swift motion the knight darted forward and thrust his sword. It would have been a dangerous blow, but Faran, though he did not anticipate it coming, still reacted with speed himself.

He rocked his weight onto the back foot and avoided the blow, but he had not retreated. Transferring his weight forward again, he launched his own counterattack, slashing at the neck of his opponent where there was a weak spot between helm and chainmail.

The blow did not land. His opponent gracefully stepped aside, avoided the blow and stabbed his own blade forward again, this time at Faran's head.

Steel crashed against steel, and sparks flew off blades. Faran blocked the attack, just barely, and launched into a vicious assault.

The two combatants traded blows. Each fought with controlled fury, like a fire burning inside ice. At first, Faran thought he was a chance of winning. He had this knight's measure. But slowly and surely his enemy wore him down. He was that little bit faster. That little bit more skilled. And the longer they fought the more those advantages told.

At length, Faran had been struck glancing blows along both arms and to his helm. None were killing blows, but together they would have weakened him in a real fight. In such a case, he would be dead now.

The knight came for him once more, those intelligent eyes cool but not without pity. Yet determination glinted in them, and Faran knew that he had given up too soon. Had he the determination of this man, he might find a way to win despite his situation.

But he did not. Soon after, he felt searing pain as the great sword of the knight hammered into his helm. From a blow such as that, he would be disabled in real life and vulnerable to any attack. Even the illusory blow stunned him, such was the nature of the magic Aranloth had wrought.

He staggered back, and when his vision cleared he saw that the knight was standing at ease, his sword dropped low.

"The fight is over," Aranloth said.

Faran nodded grudgingly and went to sit down. "Your turn, Ferla," he said.

Ferla barely looked at him. Her face was a mask of determination, and her eyes hard as diamonds. She was better than him, and just maybe she would win here when he had not. It would be a great feat, given that this was a Kingshield Knight.

Aranloth sat back to watch. So too did Faran. This would be a fight worth seeing.

The two combatants, one real and the other illusion, but seemingly as real as the other, saluted and began to circle each other.

Both looked intent and determined. For once, Ferla did not grin. And she attacked first.

Tempest Blows the Dust transformed seamlessly into Clouds Drift Across the Moon, which in turn became Stork Soars.

But her blade met only air and the cold steel of the knight's own sword. Then the knight, awaiting his chance, saw a weakness. He attacked.

Ferla retreated. Steel clanged against steel, and the sound of the swordfight rang through the valley. But Ferla remained untouched by her opponent, and in turn, seeing a weakness herself, she moved smoothly from retreat into offence.

But the knight evaded her attacks, and in turn launched his own. Thus it went back and forth, and neither could gain the ascendancy. Aranloth watched intently, and Faran watched both him and Ferla. There was determination on her face, and pride on Aranloth's. But after some time, the lòhren clapped his hands.

The knight bowed gracefully, then faded away.

Ferla did not seem happy though. "Why did you stop it? I might have won."

"Perhaps," Aranloth said. "But know this. You are flesh and blood, and grow tired. My illusions do not. The advantage was swinging toward the knight, and you deserved better than to be beaten because of that. It was a draw."

Faran went over and hugged her. "Well done!" he said.

Ferla still did not look happy. Faran knew if she had her way, she would have kept going. She would never have given up, but the lòhren was right.

"We're improving," Faran said to the old man. "That was a knight, and Ferla was not beaten by him."

Aranloth nodded slowly. "You have both come a long way in a short time. Never has anyone learned the skills of a knight as swiftly as you two. Then again, there has never been such need for it before."

Faran grinned, and even Ferla seemed to lose some of her displeasure at the fight having been stopped.

"I always give you the truth," Aranloth continued. "That is part of your training. You have done very well indeed. But you should also know the knight you fought was Lembath. He lived some three hundred years ago, and he was a good man. He was a poet, with the soul of a poet. His writings could make grown men weep, and I miss him. But he was one of the least skilled swordsman the knights have ever seen. That is simply the truth. All of the current knights would kill him swiftly in combat. Yet this is also the truth. No knight ever admitted to the kingshield order is a poor fighter. All are greatly skilled. To hold your own against one such as that is an achievement worth celebrating. I'm proud of you both, and in time you will be a match for even Lindercroft and his like."

Faran felt a surge of pride. Some was for himself, but most for Ferla. She had done better than he had. But they were both on track to obtain the skills they needed.

"Off with you now," Aranloth said. "You've had enough sword practice for one day. Time for a run, I think."

They took off, running smoothly despite the armor and sheathed swords. Aranloth had rewarded them for their good efforts, because the sword training would normally have gone on much longer.

They ran along the lake shore, which was where all their runs started from.

"Where to?" Ferla asked.

"How about the dead oak?"

They both liked it there. It was one of the best views of the valley, and that was the direction they had first seen it from.

Ferla did not answer, but nodded. They saved their breath while running, for they set a swift pace. There would be time enough to talk when they reached their destination and rested with their backs to the old tree.

Running was somewhat dangerous. The ground was often damp and slippery. But the grass was short, and the way clear.

In the little woods they passed through on their way to the ridge, it was cooler than elsewhere. Sometimes snow remained in hidden hollows, and they liked to see that. The woods were like a different world, and they reminded them of Dromdruin, which had been much more heavily forested than this valley.

They continued upward. Swallows glided and dipped through the sky. To their right, a kestrel hovered in a current of warm air, its head swiveling from side to side, its sharp eyes seeking the movement of prey below.

The land prospered under the warming sun, and the bitter nights of winter were but a memory. And as the land prospered here, so Faran felt did he and Ferla. They were more than they were. They were better than they were. Their bodies had strengthened and learned skills, while their minds had expanded.

They did not hasten, but they still moved quickly, their long strides eating up the distance. It mattered little to them if they ran uphill or downhill. It was no obstacle either way.

They wound their way up toward the dead oak. It stood by itself, though not far from a patch of woods. As always, they slowed as they reached the top of the ridge.

The ridges of the valley marked the end of their territory. Beyond here, they did not go. But more importantly, the ridges were a high point without cover. To stand there was to be seen from the wide lands all around.

They came to the dead oak, just a little below the ridgeline. As usual, they crawled over the little hill before it. The grass here was usually taller, but they still had no trouble finding enough cover to hide themselves as they peeked into the world beyond the valley.

They did so together, shoulder to shoulder, and Faran felt Ferla stiffen and go still beside him.

He went still himself, and the blood ran cold in his veins as he saw what she had seen.

24. Fire and Smoke

Peering through the grass, Faran saw a hundred or so soldiers. They were from Faladir, and mounted on a black stallion at their head was a Kingshield Knight.

And not any knight. Even at a good distance away, it was clear that the figure was Lindercroft. There was an arrogance to him, and a sense of menace that radiated from him in waves.

Ferla cursed, and together they moved back carefully through the grass until they were below the ridgeline. Ferla cursed again, more loudly, even as they broke into a run.

They headed for the closest wood. From there, they would have to be very careful to keep it between them and the enemy, lest they be seen. If that happened, a pursuit would begin and they would be caught before they could give warning to Aranloth and Kareste.

They reached the wood, but did not slow down in its cover. Once out the other side, they kept it between them and the approaching soldiers. This they would have to do with several different woods until they reached the bottom of the valley. It would take them longer this way, but they had to try to get to the cabin without being seen. That would win them more time in the end because the soldiers were only marching and not hastening. But if Lindercroft saw them, he would likely order a swift chase. For that matter, he may leave his men behind and pursue them on horseback by himself.

They were tired by the time they reached the floor of the valley. They had run as fast as they could, and they had run farther than they would normally have, seeking out woods and gulleys that hid them from view.

They hurried along the shore of the lake toward the cabin. Here, they must travel in the open, but of Lindercroft and his men there was no sign. They must have entered a wood, and that made sense because they would try to approach unseen.

Aranloth stood in the cabin doorway. He must have seen them approach and read urgency in their manner.

"What is it?" he asked.

"Lindercroft," Faran answered. "And a hundred soldiers. They're coming into the valley."

Aranloth showed no surprise. "I knew he would find us, but I had hoped for more time than this." He looked them over. "This will be difficult. But come inside and be ready."

"Inside?" Faran asked. "Surely we should run while we have the chance."

"I think not. He has found us, and he will have more forces coming in than you have seen. Probably, there are four separate groups approaching from each side. He won't be taking any chances."

That was a shock to Faran, but he should have seen it coming. That would be the way to do it, but he had never had command of men, and despite his training it was all theory. He was just not used to the idea of having hundreds of men at his disposal.

They went inside. Kareste was there, and she had heard the news.

"Quickly," she said. "Gather food supplies and water. Then be ready."

Faran and Ferla did as asked. But first they strung their bows. They could not beat all these soldiers and Lindercroft as well, but they would not go down without a fight.

It seemed to Faran that gathering supplies was a waste of time. They were trapped here, and there could be no escape. Unless Aranloth was going to use some sort of illusion to disguise them and get them out. But that could hardly work. If nothing else, Lindercroft would be aware of Aranloth's magic and on guard against it.

By the time they were ready, Lindercroft and his men were close. Aranloth was watching them through the small window near the door. Faran looked over his shoulder, and his heart sank. The old man had been right. There were more soldiers here now than they had seen before.

"We can't hold the cabin against them all," he said.

"Courage," the old man replied. "The cabin is better designed than you know."

Faran gave no answer to that. Did the old man mean the wards? But they were known to him and Ferla, and he did not think they would provide protection against normal attacks by the soldiers.

Lindercroft and his men drew close to the cabin. It burned Faran's soul that they did so. These men were murderers. Certainly Lindercroft was. His very presence defiled the valley.

"Come forth," Lindercroft demanded. "The game is up. You led me a merry chase, but now you are caught. There is no escape. You will die here. Or, you can beg my mercy. Even you, Aranloth. I am not without pity."

Aranloth did what Faran least expected. He laughed, and opened the door.

"You have no pity, Lindercroft. You have no say in anything. You are a tool. You live to serve the king, and his will is yours. And the king's will, in turn, now belongs to the Morleth Stone. Look deep into your heart, and you will see that it is so."

"It is *not* so," Lindercroft said quietly. "I am a *knight*. And I need not listen to lies from your mouth."

"Lies? How easily lies spring from your own tongue. Your orders are to kill us. Therefore, in the name of King Conduil, founder of the knights, and by my right as Osahka, I strip you of your title. You are a Kingshield Knight no longer. You are cast from the order. I judge you unworthy, and may the land have mercy upon you."

Lindercroft went white. He trembled, and Aranloth's words seemed to cut him to the bone. But the old man was not done.

"This choice is now yours, Lindercroft. You are no longer a knight. But you can redeem yourself, if you are strong enough. Renounce the king. Renounce the Shadow. Serve the Light instead."

Lindercroft swayed, and almost Faran thought the words of the lòhren might come to fruition.

But they did not. Slowly, Lindercroft shook his head in denial.

"My choices are made. My path is set, and it is unalterable." His voice grew stronger as he went on. "The king leads, and I follow. I must follow, for I have sworn to do so, and the glory of Faladir, and Alithoras after, awaits."

"You swore other oaths once," Aranloth said quietly.

"Not on the Morleth Stone. But enough of this. You are surrounded here, and there is no escape. Come out now, and die a swift death by sword, or I will burn you inside the cabin and you will perish in fire and agony."

Aranloth was not done. "I see by the scars on your face that the king is a harsher leader than ever I was or the kings before him. If you fail here, and you *will* fail here, I expect he will punish you even more harshly. He—"

"Enough!" Lindercroft signaled to his men, and Faran saw that some of them carried branches. These they set alight.

"This is your last chance, Aranloth. Come out, and bring the others with you."

"It was a last chance indeed," Aranloth replied. "But it was yours." With that, he closed the door on Lindercroft.

Aranloth looked at Kareste. "You know what to do," he said. It was not a question.

She nodded. "Good luck, old man." Strangely, she went to the table and moved it. Faran thought she meant to use it to barricade the door, but then she got on her hands and knees, drew a knife, and dug into the hardpacked clay.

It was not long before she found what she sought. She exposed a metal ring, and then she sheathed her knife and with a grunt pulled the ring hard.

The clay of the floor split in the neat form of a square, and she lifted a trapdoor upward, exposing a hole beneath, and Faran caught a glimpse of a dark tunnel. He could not believe it. All this time there had been an escape route, and he had never known of it.

"Quickly," Kareste said. "Gather your things and follow me down."

Ferla went down after her, and Faran followed. There was a sturdy ladder that went a short way and brought them to a tunnel. Wooden beams secured it, though it was narrow. But it ran arrow straight, so far as Faran could tell, toward the lake.

Light burned now at the tip of Kareste's staff. "Let's go," she said.

Faran glanced up. Aranloth had not followed them.

Kareste saw where he was looking and shook her head.

"Move! He'll join us later. For the moment, he'll stay in the cabin and ensure they don't break in too quickly. He's giving us time to escape."

"But how will *he* escape?" Ferla asked.

"He'll join us in a little while. When he's sure we're through, he'll follow, collapse the tunnel behind us and catch up. But he must make sure they don't follow. Now move!"

They hastened ahead, Kareste following up the rear. The earth seemed moist, and it grew wetter as they got closer to the lake. Soon, they were walking in pools of water, and Faran spotted an area of the tunnel that had more wooden bracing than the rest. Yet there were chains attached to that bracing, and he guessed this was where Aranloth would collapse the ceiling and prevent pursuit.

The collapse point was near the end of the tunnel. Shortly after, they climbed a set of earth stairs lined with hardwood, and Kareste slipped through ahead of them. She held a finger to her lips.

"Quiet," she whispered. "Our enemies should all be near the cabin, but this part may be dangerous."

There did not seem to be any light other than Kareste's staff, so Faran was not sure where the exit was. But at the top of the stairs was a small boat. Kareste moved beyond it, and then she traced her hands across what seemed to be a wall.

But it was not a wall. After some moments he realized it was cowhide, the thick leather heavily oiled to protect it from weather.

The light faded away from Kareste's staff, but she had gently eased the cowhide open from the bottom, and light showed from outside.

Very carefully, Kareste eased herself through and looked outside. Then she came back in.

"It's safe. At least for the moment. But be very quiet. The cabin is not so far away. Push the boat through gently, and ease it into the water. Without a splash."

She removed the cowhide from the entrance, and Faran and Ferla pushed the boat ahead. It was placed on a series of poles, and it rolled noiselessly.

Just outside the entrance, there was an overhang of willow roots, and tall reeds growing thickly. The boat moved easily through this, and then floated as water buoyed it up from underneath.

Peering just above the reeds, they saw the cabin. Flames ate it. Smoke billowed into the sky.

Faran felt tears wet his cheeks. The reek of the burning took him back to Dromdruin and murder, and he wondered if he were destined to see all that he ever loved destroyed. Once more, happiness had been taken from him. He almost ran to attack those who had done it, but that would be suicide.

He felt Ferla's hand on his shoulder. She understood. She *knew* how he felt. He glanced at Kareste. She stood close by, but her gaze was on the exit from the tunnel.

So they waited, and every breath seemed an eternity. Where was Aranloth? The sooner he came the sooner they could escape.

There was a rumble through the earth, and a few moments later a cloud of dust wafted from the tunnel exit. It could not be long now before the lòhren reached them.

But they waited in vain. The old man did not come, and the moments passed by as smoke filled the air and the cabin burned.

"Stay here," Kareste whispered. "Do not move unless the enemy comes."

So saying, she slipped back through the reeds and into the tunnel.

Faran felt a sense of dread creep over him. It was a day of destruction and doom, and he feared for the old man.

There was movement in the tunnel a few moments later. It was Kareste, and her face was coated by dust and she coughed quietly.

"Move," she hissed. "Row the boat toward the center of the lake."

"What of Aranloth?" Ferla asked.

"He must be dead. He triggered the trap from the *other* side and blocked off pursuit. They must have come into the cabin too quickly for him to make good his escape."

"Then we have to go back for him to be sure."

"He's beyond our help. Don't let his sacrifice be in vain. Now into the boat and row. The time he bought us so dearly slips away!"

Reluctantly, they boarded the boat and used the paddles stored within it to row. Faran felt cold shock. Aranloth was dead. If he were on this side of the collapsed tunnel, Kareste would have found him. On the other side, he would surely be killed by Lindercroft and all his men.

There was no choice but to go on. Kareste drew a mist up from the water to hide them, and dispersed it gently between them and the shore. It was not a thick fog. It was enough to hide them only, but not so much as to attract attention.

Lindercroft and his men would have to wait a long time for the burning cabin to cool down. Only then could they go in and check for bodies.

It worried Faran that they may have discovered the tunnel. If that were so, then they would start to search immediately. But there was no sign of that. Aranloth must have triggered the collapse by magic, and then stayed in the cabin for a last stand.

He realized that Ferla was crying, and he put an arm around her.

"What do we do now?" he asked Kareste.

"We escape, as Aranloth wanted us to. And then your training continues."

Faran felt a cold determination grow inside him. Twice now, his enemies had murdered by fire and steel those he knew. Twice now, they had stolen happiness from him.

He would learn what he must. Nothing would stop him, and then he would find a way to destroy Lindercroft. And after him, even the king, no matter that he was protected by his knights and an army. Nor even the power of the Morleth Stone…

Thus ends *The Sorcerer Knight.* The Kingshield series continues in book three, *The Sage Knight*, where Faran and Ferla discover more of the arts of the knights, and the shadow of the Morleth Stone stretches longer…

THE SAGE KNIGHT

BOOK THREE OF THE KINGSHIELD SERIES

Amazon lists millions of titles, and I'm glad you discovered this one. But if you'd like to know when I release a new book, instead of leaving it to chance, sign up for my new release list. I'll send you an email on publication.

Yes please! – Go to www.homeofhighfantasy.com and sign up.

No thanks – I'll take my chances.

Dedication

There's a growing movement in fantasy literature. Its name is noblebright, and it's the opposite of grimdark.

Noblebright celebrates the virtues of heroism. It's an old-fashioned thing, as old as the first story ever told around a smoky campfire beneath ancient stars. It's storytelling that highlights courage and loyalty and hope for the spirit of humanity. It recognizes the dark, the dark in us all, and the dark in the villains of its stories. It recognizes death, and treachery and betrayal. But it dwells on none of these things.

I dedicate this book, such as it is, to that which is noblebright. And I thank the authors before me who held the torch high so that I could see the path: J.R.R. Tolkien, C.S. Lewis, Terry Brooks, David Eddings, Susan Cooper, Roger Taylor and many others. I salute you.

And, for a time, I too shall hold the torch high.

Appendix: Encyclopedic Glossary

Note: the glossary of each book in this series is individualized for that book alone. Additionally, there is often historical material provided in its entries for people, artifacts and events that are not included in the main text.

Many races dwell in Alithoras. All have their own language, and though sometimes related to one another the changes sparked by migration, isolation and various influences often render these tongues unintelligible to each other.

The ascendancy of Halathrin culture, combined with their widespread efforts to secure and maintain allies against elug incursions, has made their language the primary means of communication between diverse peoples.

This glossary contains a range of names and terms. Many are of Halathrin origin, and their meaning is provided. The remainder derive from native tongues and are obscure, so meanings are only given intermittently.

Often, names of Camar and Halathrin elements are combined. This is especially so for the aristocracy. Few other tribes had such long-term friendship with the immortal Halathrin as the Camar, and though in this relationship they lost some of their natural culture, they gained nobility and knowledge in return.

List of abbreviations:

Cam. Camar

Comb. Combined

Cor. Corrupted form

Hal. Halathrin

Leth. Letharn

Prn. Pronounced

Alithoras: *Hal.* "Silver land." The Halathrin name for the continent they settled after leaving their own homeland. Refers to the extensive river and lake systems they found and their wonder at the beauty of the land.

Aranloth: *Hal.* "Noble might." A lòhren of ancient heritage. Travels Alithoras under different names and guises.

Brand: *Duth.* A heroic figure in Alithoras. Both warrior and lòhren. Stories of his exploits have spread over the land, and they kindle hope wherever they are heard.

Camar: *Cam. Prn.* Kay-mar. A race of interrelated tribes that migrated in two main stages. The first brought them to the vicinity of Halathar, homeland of the immortal Halathrin; in the second, they separated and established cities along a broad stretch of eastern Alithoras. Faladir is one such city.

Camarelon: *Cam.* A city established by migrating Camar tribes. Its people retained more of their traditional cultural values and were less influenced by the Halathrin. The city they built is not as grand as other Camar cities, but it still became wealthy via profitable trade.

Carcur-halioth: *Leth.* An ancient circle of standing stones constructed by the Letharn. Named after one of their great magicians, Carcur. His abode was in Arach Nedular, but he had great need to travel widely through the Letharn empire, which was vast. He did not invent Traveling, but he discovered how to construct a Ring that made the process far less dangerous.

Cardoroth: *Cor. Hal. Comb. Cam.* A Camar city, often called Red Cardoroth. Some say this alludes to the red granite commonly used in the construction of its buildings, others that it refers to a prophecy of destruction. If so, Brand appears to have thwarted it.

Careth Tar: *Cor. Hal.* "Careth Tar(an) – Great Father." Title of respect for the leader of the lòhrens. This has always been, and remains, Aranloth.

Conduil: *Cam.* Etymology obscure. The first king of Faladir. He broke the Siege of Faladir and founded the order of Kingshield Knights, of which he was the first. Among his descendants there is a high prevalence of knights.

Dromdruin: *Cam.* "Valley of the ancient woods." One of many valleys in the realm of Faladir. Home of Faran, and birthplace throughout the history of the realm of many Kingshield Knights.

Druilgar: *Hal.* "Spear star – a comet." King of Faladir, and First Knight of the Kingshield Knights. Descendent of King Conduil.

Duthenor: *Duth.* "The people." A tribe of people farther to the west of Camar lands. Related to the Camar, and sharing many common legends and experiences. But different also.

Elves: See Halathrin.

Elù-drak: *Hal.* "Shadow wings." A creature of the dark. Deadly, and used by sorcerers to gather information and assassinate chosen victims. The female of the species is the most dangerous, having the power to inspire terror and bend victims to her will. Few can resist. Of old, even great warriors succumbed and willingly let the creature take their life. One of the more terrible creatures of the Old World.

Elùdurlik: *Hal.* "Shadow hunter." A type of summoning. Formed of a melding of dark magic and the thoughts of the summoner. Instilled with a driving purpose that it can never ignore, and dies once that purpose is achieved.

Elùgai: *Hal. Prn.* Eloo-guy. "Shadowed force." The sorcery of an elùgroth.

Elù-haraken: *Hal.* "The shadowed wars." Long ago battles in a time that is become myth to the scattered Camar tribes.

Elùdrath: *Hal.* "Shadowed lord." Once, a lòhren. But he succumbed to evil and pursued forbidden knowledge and powers. He created an empire of darkness and struck to conquer all Alithoras during the elù-haraken. He was defeated, but his magic had become greater than any ever known. Some say he will return from death to finish the war he started. Whether that is so, no one knows. But the order of lòhrens guard against it, and many evils that served him yet live.

Elùgroth: *Hal.* "Shadowed horror." A sorcerer. They often take names in the Halathrin tongue in mockery of the lòhren practice to do so.

Faladir: *Cam.* "Fortress of Light." A Camar city founded out of the ruinous days of the elù-haraken.

Faran: *Cam.* "Spear of the night – a star." A name of good luck. Related to the name Dardenath, though of a later layer of linguistic change. A young hunter from Dromdruin valley. His grandfather was a Kingshield Knight, though not the first of their ancestors to be so.

Ferla: *Cam.* "Unforeseen bounty." A young hunter from Dromdruin valley.

First Knight: The designated leader of the Kingshield Knights.

Gaeblung: A general of antiquity. Said to be a Duthenor warrior, though his mother was of the Camar. His skill in the art of warfare was so great that even the Halathrin gave command of some of their armies to him. A forefather of Brand.

Halathrin: *Hal.* "People of Halath." A race of elves named after an honored lord who led an exodus of his people to the land of Alithoras in pursuit of justice, having sworn to defeat a great evil. They are human, though of fairer form, greater skill and higher culture. They possess a unity of body, mind and spirit that enables insight and endurance beyond the native races of Alithoras. Said to be immortal, but killed in great numbers during their conflicts in ancient times with the evil they sought to destroy. Those conflicts are collectively known as the Shadowed Wars.

Halakness: A word of power. It means water. Used to focus the mind in the early stages of lòhrengai. In truth, no words of power are needed for magic. Their usage is a beginner's aid.

Haeldurn: A word of power. It means to protect, to cause to endure or to remain steadfast.

Har-harat: *Leth.* An energy point of the body just below the navel. Used as a focus for meditation and to replenish the body's vital force. By meditation on this point, the physical body and the spiritual essence are unified. Used by both warriors and mystics.

Harakgar: *Leth.* "The three sisters." Creatures of magic brought into being by the Letharn. Their purpose is to protect the tombs of their creators from robbery.

Hrokhar: A word of power. It signifies warmth.

Immortals: See Halathrin.

Jareck: Etymology obscure. A trader, storyteller and tinker. Was once a lòhren, but is so no more. Yet he remains a trusted friend of Aranloth.

Kareste: *Hal.* "Ice unlocking – the spring thaw." A lòhren of mysterious origin. Friend to Aranloth, but usually more active farther north in Alithoras than Faladir.

Kasellah: *Leth.* "The follower who learns – a disciple." A student of an Osahka.

Kingshield Knights: An order of knights founded by King Conduil. Their sacred task is to guard the indestructible Morleth Stone from theft and use by the evil forces of the world. They are more than great warriors, being trained in philosophy and the arts also. In addition to their prime function as guards, they travel the land at whiles dispensing justice and offering of their wisdom and council.

Lady of the Land: The spirit of the land. It is she whom lòhrens serve, though her existence is seldom discussed.

Lanrik: Leader of the Raithlin organization of scouts. A hero of great renown in Alithoras.

Lembath: *Hal.* "Flight of a dove." A member of Faladir royalty and a Kingshield Knight of several hundred years ago. Famed also as a poet, and his ballads in honor of his friend Aranloth are still recited throughout the kingdom, and beyond.

Letharn: *Hal.* "Stone raisers. Builders." A race of people that in antiquity conquered most of Alithoras. Now, only faint traces of their civilization endure.

Lindercroft: *Cam.* "Rising mountain crashes – a wave rolling into the seashore." A Kingshield Knight. Youngest of the order.

Lòhren: *Hal. Prn.* Ler-ren. "Knowledge giver – a counselor." Other terms used by various nations include wizard, druid and sage.

Lòhren-fire: A defensive manifestation of lòhrengai. The color of the flame varies according to the skill and temperament of the lòhren.

Lòhrengai: *Hal. Prn.* Ler-ren-guy. "Lòhren force." Enchantment, spell or use of mystic power. A manipulation and transformation of the natural energy inherent in all things. Each use takes something from the user. Likewise, some part of the transformed energy infuses them. Lòhrens use it sparingly, elùgroths indiscriminately.

Magic: Mystic power. See lòhrengai and elùgai.

Morleth Stone: *Hal.* "Round stone." The name signifies that such a stone is not natural. It is formed by elùgai for sorcerous purposes. The stone is strengthened by arcane power to act as a receptacle of enormous force. Little is known of their making and uses except that they are rare and that elùgroths perish during their construction. The stone guarded by the Kingshield Knights in Faladir is said to be the most powerful of all that were created. And to be sentient.

Nuatha: *Cam.* "Silver wanderer – a stream." A vagabond healer who travels widely throughout Faladir.

Nurthil Wood: *Cam.* "Dark secrets." A great forest north of Faladir. Home to outlaws and disaffected from the wide lands all around. Once a stronghold of the forces of darkness, but cleansed by succeeding kings of Faladir.

Olek-nas: *Leth.* "The third eye." An energy point on the body between the eyebrows. Maintained to be a center of rationality and calm. Once a practitioner of the meditative arts "opens" this energy center, they are said to be able to look upon the world and see it for what it is with emotional detachment. Used in both the mystic and the warrior arts.

Osahka: *Leth.* "The guide – specifically a spiritual or moral guide." A title of enormous reverence and respect. Applied to Aranloth for his role as spiritual leader of the Kingshield Knights.

Raithlin: *Hal.* "Range and report people." A scouting and saboteur organization. Famed for their skills.

Savanest: *Cam.* "Subtle skill." A Kingshield Knight.

Shadowed Wars: See Elù-haraken.

Sorcerer: See Elùgroth.

Sorcery: See elùgai.

Tallach-far: The ancient city at the heart of the Letharn empire.

Three sisters, the: See harakgar.

Tower of the Stone: The tower King Conduil caused to be built to serve as the guarding structure of the Morleth Stone. Some claim his sarcophagus rests upon its pinnacle, as it was the custom of some ancient Camar royalty to be interred on a high place where the lights of the sun, moon and stars still lit their long sleep.

Traveling: A feat of lòhrengai of the highest order. It enables movement of the physical body from one location to another via entry to the void in one place and exit in a different. Only the greatest wizards are capable of it, but it is never used. The risk of death is too high. But use of specially constructed rings of standing stones makes it safer.

Ùhrengai: *Hal.* "Original force." The primordial force that existed before substance or time.

Way of the Sword: The martial aspect of the training of a Kingshield Knight.

Wizard: See lòhren.

About the author

I'm a man born in the wrong era. My heart yearns for faraway places and even further afield times. Tolkien had me at the beginning of *The Hobbit* when he said, ". . . one morning long ago in the quiet of the world . . ."

Sometimes I imagine myself in a Viking mead-hall. The long winter night presses in, but the shimmering embers of a log in the hearth hold back both cold and dark. The chieftain calls for a story, and I take a sip from my drinking horn and stand up . . .

Or maybe the desert stars shine bright and clear, obscured occasionally by wisps of smoke from burning camel dung. A dry gust of wind marches sand grains across our lonely campsite, and the wayfarers about me stir restlessly. I sip cool water and begin to speak.

I'm a storyteller. A man to paint a picture by the slow music of words. I like to bring faraway places and times to life, to make hearts yearn for something they can never have, unless for a passing moment.

Printed in Great Britain
by Amazon